PISTOL ROSE

and the Wedding that Sparked a War

Book I of
The Anthem of Ash & Pistols

by
Michael Ryan Hahn

To Renee,
All my best, Mike Hahn

SWASH
BUCKLE
HOLDINGS

ISBN: 978-1-962089-00-5 (paperback)
ISBN 978-1-962089-01-2 (ebook)
Library of Congress Control Number: 2023913514

Cover design and all artwork created by Michael Ryan Hahn.

No Artificial Intelligence was used

Printed in Los Angeles, California, USA
First Printing August 2023
Published by Swashbuckle Holdings

Visit www.michaelryanhahn.com

For Dad, the truest Punimin

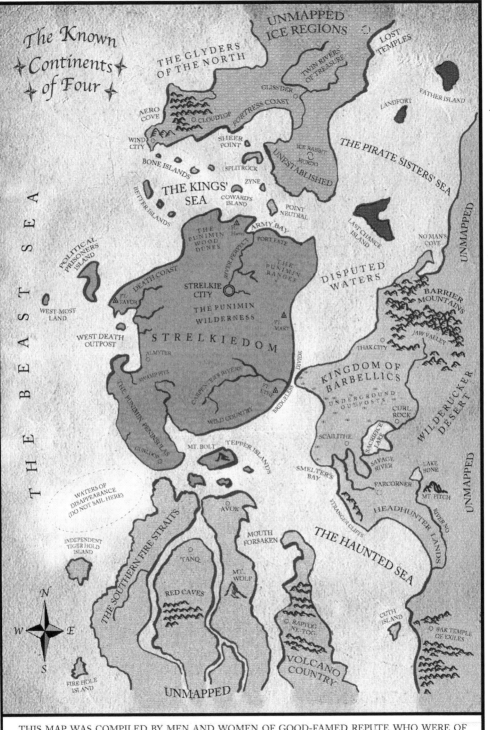

The Known
✦ Continents ✦
✦ of Four ✦

UNMAPPED
ICE REGIONS

LOST
TEMPLES

THE GLYDERS
OF THE NORTH

TWIN RIVERS
OF TREASURE

GLISS'DER

FATHER ISLAND

LANDFORT

AERO
COVE

O. CLOUDTOP

FORTRESS COAST

WIND
CITY

SHEER
POINT

THE PIRATE SISTERS' SEA

ICE RABBIT

O MURDO

UNESTABLISHED

BONE ISLANDS

SPLITROCK

THE KINGS'
SEA

ZYNE

HETTER ISLANDS

COWARD'S
ISLAND

POINT
NEUTRAL

NO MAN'S
COVE

ARMY BAY

LAST CHANCE
ISLAND

THE BEAST SEA

POLITICAL
PRISONERS
ISLAND

THE
PUNIMIN
WOOD
DUNES

Harno

PORT FATE

DISPUTED
WATERS

BARRIER
MOUNTAINS

RIVER SERVICE

THE
PUNIMIN
RANGES

DEATH COAST

FT. FAVOR

STRELKIE
CITY

UNMAPPED

WEST-MOST
LAND

THE PUNIMIN
WILDERNESS

JAW VALLEY

MT.
MARY

WEST DEATH
OUTPOST

S T R E L K I E D O M

THAK CITY

ALMYTER

SWAMP PITS

KINGDOM OF
BARBELLICS

CARPENTER'S RIVER

UNDERGROUND
OUTPOSTS

CURL
ROCK

THE PUNIMIN PENINSULAS

FT.
ETHE

WILD COUNTRY

BRIDGELESS DIVIDE

WILDERUCKER
DESERT

SCAILITHE

SACRIFICE
LAKE

GUNLOCK

MT. BOLT

TEPPER ISLANDS

SMELTER'S
BAY

SAVAGE
RIVER

LAKE
BONE

FARCORNER

MT. PITCH

WATERS OF
DISAPPEARANCE
(DO NOT SAIL HERE)

AVOK

STRANGER CLIFFS

HEADHUNTER
LANDS

UNMAPPED

INDEPENDENT
TIGER HOLD
ISLAND

MOUTH
FORSAKEN

THE HAUNTED SEA

RIVER NO

N

TANQ

MT.
WOLF

THE SOUTHERN FIRE STRAITS

W E

RED CAVES

CUTH
ISLAND

S

O RAPTOG
NE-TOG

O BAK TEMPLE
OF EXILES

FIRE HOLE
ISLAND

VOLCANO
COUNTRY

UNMAPPED

THIS MAP WAS COMPILED BY MEN AND WOMEN OF GOOD-FAMED REPUTE WHO WERE OF
COUNSEL TO TOIR-PAT, KEPT CAREFUL RECORDS AND MEASUREMENTS, AND CONSIDERED
HISTORICAL MAPS IN THEIR COLLABORATION TO RENDER THIS MODERN UNDERSTANDING.

Pistol Family

Grace - David   Madrick - (Callory)

Rose   Jennifer   Ann   Beau

Clock Family

Francine - Wyatt

Leslie - Rollo

Ejjer   Dancin   Zoe

PISTOL ROSE

and the Wedding that Sparked a War

*A tale rendered true by one who lived through the
times and knew the heroes*

Though this story happened many years ago at the end of the Fifth Age, I still see it crisply when I close my eyes. They were my friends, and I came to love them—even if I was stubborn about it. Their story is alive. To me it is now, and it is always. This is how I tell it.

A warning: this work offers a glimpse into the Four Continents of the Known World, and life as it was before the Revolution. Those days were built upon long-disputed histories and dark mysteries, on the noble barbarians and murderous poets who raised an empire on the heaps of bones and the tongues of cheats. Many are the thought-trappers who to this day dispute the nature of our world's foundation, but their exaggerations are designed to weave you astray. Beware the "carvers," meaning "liars who edit or twist," the foulest of all people. Such agenda'd fingers shall not corrupt this rendering. Here I present—freely and honestly—the raw truth about folk like Pistol Rose and Clock Dancin, the warrior-heroes of my tale. They carried hearts of gold and fists of nails, and I blink at none of it.

My story is my memory, and a swift arrow. I light it now. The flames dance like a racing thought out of time. I nock it and pull the string; the limbs bow back and groan; I loose the shaft and its tip of fire soars as a falcon. We must sprint to follow, or miss its tale!

For that is how I see this story, even now. I am as a scribe, alive and present.

I am young again.

I am there.

Fly with me.

CHAPTER I

LILLY'S LIFE

You have gathered with me to hear the story of Pistol Rose ... and the trouble she made. She was raised in a dangerous time, made even more dangerous by the fact of her life and what she did with it. To this day, many people who weren't there call me a lying carver. Such is the way of cowards and tyrants. But I knew Pistol Rose. As did a young girl named Lilly.

The isolated old city of glass and gold shimmers on the horizon like a jewel in an endless forest wilderness. Strelkie City is an ageless feat of engineering, a breathing gift from the future, or so its dwellers say. Every day some new advanced technology is whispered about, and every month a freshly conceived device arrives, with endless copies finding their way into the clamoring hands of the Strelkie citizenry. They are a miserable people.

Their comforts rob them—if you ask the Punimin folk who only know wilderness life. Strelkie City bars most Punimin from entry. The metropolis is walled, and it is guarded. The Strelkie like it that way; the Punimin need it—they don't want Strelkie slithering into their forest and changing their ways, as Strelkie are wont to do. The Punimin propagate rumors and carve tales of beasts, building an ever-growing lore, mostly to keep the Strelkie afraid. But they needn't worry, for Punimin life is medieval—and miserable—if you ask the Strelkie. Each side thinks the other is the victim of a dystopia masquerading as a promise of happiness.

And this is precisely how King Ward Harrol wants the Fifth Age to be. This is how he needs it to be: with all his people distracted by the perfect balance of discomfort and hope. His great city of Strelkie, surrounded by a greater vastness of his wild Punimin, is a delicate country to keep at peace. Life for the king is said to be like holding back a violent sneeze that's one hair's edge from roaring loose, and he must wield the bulk of his government's considerable power to keep it from bursting free. But even the king can't be everywhere. His control is never more fraught than on doomed days like this, where our story begins. Well, doomed for some.

A horse-drawn birthday carriage with banners of truce and an escort of Strelkie soldiers plods away from the city on a worn dirt road. The Strelkie wear red, and their armor today is fit for the arena—scaled leather under shiny steel plates engraved with counting teeth—each kill or "noble act" is recorded on their armor as a stamped tooth. They carry long guns and short swords. You might spot an occasional whip or mace. Their weapons are meant to spark imagination—how might that metal feel upon my chest if I anger a Strelkie soldier? Many curious Punimin have found out. Some such Punimin, warriors dressed in their colors of green and white, with handcrafted armor of their own that has less uniformity but more blacksmith skill and dirty tricks (like retractable spikes), watch this horse-drawn carriage with a show of arms from positions along the forest road among thick trees. They let the Strelkie know they're there, but they keep their true numbers hidden. Everyone is eager to land the second blow, and each fighter prays the other side lands the first to set off the excuse to battle and spill blood.

In the birthday carriage, a ten-year-old girl named Lilly, with bright red hair, sits watching the woman in charge of her: a pregnant Strelkie by the name of Wynter. Wynter is being pampered by two assistants who hold her and dab her sweat away as the old-fashioned carriage jostles and herks. She is under a traditional flinty black blanket patterned with crows on the outside and white doves on the inside to symbolize both possible outcomes of her important moment ahead, but Lilly knows the meaning is beneath Wynter. Wynter doesn't care—or isn't aware—of the symbology. Wynter isn't the kind of person who believes the black-and-white dual fortunes of everyone else apply to her. She believes she knows exactly how this day will go, one way or the other, and has planned it for some time. Just like all her days. This is simply another task.

Lilly doesn't bother to challenge Wynter's thinking as she has other women and men who've been wrong about all kinds of things—after more caregivers than Lilly can count, she knows better than to hassle adults. She's only ten and *she* knows birthing isn't easy, but best to just go along. So, she quietly stares out the window ... until her curiosity leaks out despite herself.

"Why aren't there birthday hospitals in Strelkie City?" Lilly asks.

Wynter replies, exhausted by months of privately fretting, "The law, Lilly. Ward Harrol knows best. Don't question." Then Wynter yells with pain that Lilly suspects both surprises and scares her. Lilly can't know Wynter's mind or true feelings because they hardly know each other at all, and they share little more than a mutual, if polite, distaste. They've been assigned together by law, and the only fortunate thing about that to Lilly is the timing. She's always wanted to see a baby come, and this one will be here soon.

Lilly catches sight of Punimin warriors watching them casually and coldly from the trees. They frighten her, these rugged brutes. Their weapons are battered and worn, unlike the Strelkie arms. It's as if the Punimin actually use theirs. Lilly scowls at them like a caged varmint—it's a learned look. When in doubt, look mean.

Birthing days on the Line are tricky. It's the only time more than several Strelkie and Punimin mix, officially. Two cultures, two nations, two peoples Ward Harrol has no desire to mingle. But he must control births this way, because he wants many sons for his armies to plunder faraway lands. If he allowed his people to decide who kept which babies, and where which children were raised, the delicate balance upon which his power rests would be knocked askew. And he hasn't ruled for as impressively long as he has by letting anything like that happen. Not even once.

Lilly holds on tight as the carriage bounces and approaches a border hospital, a large white field tent where the dirt road ends and a Strelkie nurse waits with a Punimin nurse. The tent rests along a Line of neutral territory, by decree. The medical tools inside shine by sunlight through open tent flaps. The contraptions are largely made of wood and iron, but they are of artisan quality with smooth, clean curves and not at all uncomfortable. Steam is the fuel for anything that needs more than human hands to make it go, and the entire environment within and around the tent is humbling by design. This might be neutral territory, but when you're here, your service to the king is that much more important. Everyone is as an animal in this place, a pet out to prove its obedience, and eyes are watching like tax counters. Lilly is excited by every fascinating detail she sees. Seldom have ten-year-olds gotten to attend a birthing day.

For those Strelkie who love the king, these border hospitals are hallowed ground. For Punimin and for those Strelkie who secretly despise him—and those Strelkie exist—these tents are a necessary evil to be tolerated. Anything to win favor instead of unwanted attention.

Wynter's assistants help her out of the carriage. She walks and wibbles like her knees have forgotten how to hinge. "Stay here, Lilly," she says.

"In the carriage?" Lilly asks. She thought she was going to get to come inside.

"Yes. Stay fixed here. I might need you. Don't wander; there are frights in the wilderness that will kill you." Wynter snaps her fingers loudly in Lilly's face to emphasize the threat.

The assistants help Wynter hobble to the nurses. Lilly immediately sneaks out of the carriage to explore like a darting hummingbird with sharp bursts and quick pauses to stay out of sight. She creeps past Punimin warriors and peeks through a split in the tent to behold the maternity ward, empty of patients and babies, but not of nurses. From her view she can only see feet.

Suddenly hands burst out of the tent and drag her inside—

The hands belong to a young Pistol Rose. She's ten, just like Lilly, but a light-haired young Punimin with piercing eyes. She motions for Lilly to hush and hides with her under a bed. They're complete strangers.

"Are you a Strelkie?" Rose asks.

"Yes. Are you a Punimin?" Lilly whispers.

Rose shows a brand on the back of her hand: the mark of all Punimin born on the Line. It looks like an old burn scar from a key in the shape of a skull.

It frightens Lilly. "Are you going to eat me?"

"What? No." Rose looks incredulous.

"But I heard Punimin eat meat."

"Not people meat," Rose frowns. "I heard Strelkie are stupid and hate all Punimin."

"Not me. I'm Lilly."

"I'm Pistol Rose. My mom's Pistol Grace. She's a nurse's assistant. Want to be friends?"

Lilly considers, then nods. Rose ties a small friendship bracelet made of wooden beads and petrified nuts onto Lilly's wrist. Lilly offers her a wooden glove with mechanical fingers.

"What's that?" Rose asks.

"It's a citizen glove. It keeps your hands clean and distant from the things you touch, there's a quality sensor for prices so you don't have to look at tags, and when you're in food shops it keeps people from stealing because the fingers lock open. It's very popular with good people right now."

"I don't want that."

"Oh." Lilly looks worried. "Then I don't have anything to give you for the bracelet."

Rose shrugs. "You'll think of something someday." She trades a smile with Lilly and lets those words hang.

Suddenly Wynter yells like the world is tearing apart. Hers is. Nurse feet shuffle and voices climb on top of each other with a panic. Lilly tries to watch as instructions are hastily yelled and Wynter calms a little. The fracas subdues and gives way to firm coaching talk, and from what the girls can see the now-calmed feet make it look like this procedure is going roughly as it should.

"Whoa," Lilly whispers.

Rose asks, "Is it true Strelkie don't have dads?"

Lilly nods. "Strelkie don't have dads or moms. No families. It's the law."

Rose frowns. "So, everyone in the city lives alone?"

"No, we live in groups." Lilly is happy to share. "Everybody rotates every three months. It's on a cycle. One child per two adults. Families are a threat to Civil Unity. How do you Punimin do it?"

"Families."

A new baby cries. "It's a boy," one of the nurses says dryly. Rose and Lilly strain to see but can't quite, as Wynter asks, "May I hold him? ... What's wrong?"

Rose senses trouble. She taps Lilly to leave with her. Lilly shakes her head no.

A nurse proclaims, "The neutral examiner has determined this case has a defect."

Lilly's eyes get big with worry.

Rose tugs on her. "You have to go now."

Wynter sounds pained, like a traveler who has been told her boat is leaving without her. "No, no. He looks fine."

Rose can't get Lilly to budge. A nurse says, "He is too big. He will not be permitted to live in Strelkie City. Strelkie citizens are small and efficient. To the Punimin fall the excess."

Lilly catches a glimpse of a nurse branding the newborn's hand with a red-hot key. The baby screams with a shrill violence none here will ever forget. He swats the key loose and it skitters under a bed.

"I didn't get the mark on him," a nurse says. "Where'd that key go?"

Lilly looks to Rose's brand. It's the same mark, of a skull.

Wynter shouts, "No! Don't mark him! He's not Punimin! He's Strelkie like me! Please!" She falls to the floorboards and clutches at a nurse. Lilly and Rose see Wynter, but she doesn't see them. "I'll trade you!" Wynter screams, "I brought a Strelkie girl! Lilly. In five years, she can give you many babies. Please give me my boy!" And just like that, Wynter's plan comes to light.

Lilly suddenly realizes why she was brought here. Why the normally cruel Wynter was so kind to her these last several weeks. This isn't a "special trip" at all. It's a trap. Lilly looks horrified.

Then Wynter sees them hiding under the bed. She points at Lilly and shrieks, "There she is! Take her instead! Take her!"

Rose pulls Lilly away. They flee into the forest outside the tent.

But a Strelkie soldier spots them. "You there! Stop!"

Rose leads Lilly to a river. They flit and race like mad foxes, ducking under branches and winding through tight gaps between bushes. They narrowly fit and squeeze through so closely that the leaves and thorns scratch their faces. Spiderwebs tangle in their eyelashes. Any soldier who might chase them will have to take a longer path to the river.

Lilly is beside herself with worry. "I can't be a Punimin! You live in huts. You eat trash. You don't have technology! That's not *comfortable!* How can Wynter do this to me?" Lilly pulls spiderwebs out of her eyes and brushes a caterpillar out of her hair. "Do you think they're really going to trade me?"

Rose stops at the river's edge. It's a broad waterway and moving fast. "I don't know. It's happened before. It's because

Strelkie get privileges if you make boys for the armies. You crazies hate girls."

"That isn't true, Rose! You don't know anything about us Strelkie! You're a stupid, backwoods defect!"

Rose knows differently. "I'm not a defect. My parents are just Punimin."

Lilly nods. "Yeah. Defect outdoor scum." She says this matter-of-factly and means no harm by it. It's just the truth she's been taught.

Rose pokes Lilly in the chest. "*Everybody* gets born in a border hospital and the *nurses* pick who's Strelkie and who's Punimin. It's about Ward Harrol keeping the city and fort populations under control. That's all. They can't even really tell defects. A 'defect' can mean anything."

Lilly won't listen to this. "No. Strelkie are better. Punimin-born never go to the city, except as servants. We're advanced."

"You're all scrawny psychopaths," Rose says as though gently breaking news.

"No, *you're* psychopaths! You're all too tall and big and muscly to feed efficiently!" Lilly is crying.

Rose says, "We feed ourselves fine. We don't need mechanical gloves to tell us what to touch. We think for ourselves and everything."

Lilly almost hyperventilates. "Not efficiently. We're citizens! We're *good!* Ward Harrol knows; he's a god and he *loves* us. We get laws that make sense and keep us safe. But he hates you. You're barbarians—you don't even have lots of money. We're *different!*"

Rose nods. "We sure are. Can you swim, Lilly?"

"Of course. It's part of mandatory citizen train—"

Rose shoves her into the river. "That runs back to the city! Have a comfortable life, Strelkie!"

Lilly swims as two Strelkie soldiers run up to Rose, sticky with spiderwebs and leaves, out of breath, red-faced and fuming mad. Lilly stops herself in the water against a rock under some shade and turns to look back as Rose points to misdirect the soldiers upriver. They race that way, away from Lilly.

Rose and Lilly quietly watch each other. Rose waves for her to let go of the rock and swim home, but Lilly stays stuck in place, afraid to move, afraid that her red hair will give her away if she floats out of the shadows. The soldiers return, more hot than before.

The first growls, "Kill this Punimin cud for lying."

Lilly watches as the second soldier pins Rose against a tree and draws a knife—Rose jabs his eye with her thumb and he drops her. She claws her hand into his groin, twists, and he quickly finds that nothing is more important in life right now than kneeling and trying to remember how to breathe. The first soldier comes swatting at her like a lumberjack who can't reach the low tree stumps and she squeaks under his knees like a slippery beast. She's been training since before she could walk, and she walked early.

The first soldier draws a gun—Rose throws a dagger into his arm, and he stumbles into the river. He splashes and is confused at the quick glance he catches of her dagger's handle protruding from him: a carving of a three-year-old Rose choking a Strelkie soldier. He doesn't have time to consider the meaning of this—his armor is too heavy and he's sinking. "Help!"

The second soldier reaches for him—gets yanked in. They start to drown like snails stuck in the wrong shells, but grab onto a fallen tree to *just* keep their faces above water. Rose carefully reaches in at them and retrieves her dagger by yanking it out of the wounded man while avoiding their thrashing hands. It's like trying to rob an octopus without getting touched by its tentacles. Lilly holds her breath watching. Rose manages to snatch her dagger, and runs to flee—

"You'll pay for this!" the first soldier yells. "You're a *carver!*"

Rose stops at the word, "carver." That is no light insult. But after a very adult moment of self-control, she decides to let it go and leave—

The second soldier adds, "We'll execute your family in the public square!"

Rose spins around. She walks back and considers them, these gagging, pathetic monsters. She stomps on the tree. They scream. Stomp, stomp—the tree snaps in a spiral curve and the wood spews a fresh, delicious smell of raw timber that carries its scent all the way to Lilly. Then the tree breaks loose, and the men sink under it with a simple gurgle. Gone. Lilly watches bubbles breach the surface for a moment, then stop.

"No, you won't," Rose says. She runs away, deeper into the wilderness.

Lilly has never met a family before, but she wonders what about it could be so important to make Rose kill those men who threatened hers. Rose didn't even hesitate. That little Punimin girl turned into a coldblooded warrior and struck with the certainty and precision of a clock—a tiny hand ticking with the power of time. With the power to end it, for those men. And now she's gone.

Lilly lets go of the rock and the river drives her away. Her shining red hair looks like a wet torch bobbing as a raft, brightly lighting her homeward to a future that she can't know and is afraid to imagine right now. Whatever happens, Strelkiedom will never look the same to her again. Few days will pass in the next ten years where Lilly doesn't think about this day and Pistol Rose, where she doesn't wonder if they'll meet again.

Though Rose is Lilly's opposite in most ways and will spend much less time reckoning back on this particular day—many of her days are filled with danger and Punimin adventuring—she does share something in common with Lilly. Neither girl realizes the great significance their chance childhood meeting will later bear on the fate of their adult lives—and on their country.

CHAPTER  II

KING'S LAW

W hile Strelkie and Punimin couldn't be more different (the citizens in the city are generally small, where the Punimin are often larger and stronger), they share one king and, therefore, one source of technological gift-rendering. Their cultures only overlap in the slightest, most controlled of ways, but gadgets from the city often land in the calloused fingers of crafty Punimin who repurpose and improve them—automatic hair-combers make the best flowerpot sifters; mechanical weather-predictors are easily repurposed into sirens to frighten off garden crows; the tiny screens found in most Strelkie hands at all hours of the day are easily smashed into sparkling jewelry. Even if the "improvements" to Strelkie gadgets fail, it's the act of changing them that counts most to Punimin. It's widely said that if Punimin dying of thirst found Strelkie water, their first act would be to see if it could be set on fire.

Though many Punimin wear jewelry hewn from smashed Strelkie inventions, most jewelry is not favored among the

Punimin—in fact, it is considered elitist. But wearing a pin on your top hat or showing off a bedazzled watch, if its root is taken from the king's feeble Strelkie, is different. Such things are badges of honor, even if worn subtly. Strangers might think these are loving homages to the king, and if asked by a suspicious poker, a Punimin might even declare that—but the meaning is quite the opposite.

A few clever, or at least *willing*, Punimin work service jobs within the city's walls. Some do it for the money, some for the underground trade opportunities. Others do it because it is the closest thing to military action they can take—they get to spy on the enemy and bring news home. But such adventures find death in unexpected corners. Strelkie City is beautiful, but not without its torments and troubles, especially for Punimin who see too much.

So here, in Punimin country, the people live their own way, Strelkie-free. Punimin are subject to much of King's Law, but Strelkie rarely visit to enforce, especially not in the forest regions. Most won't dare—it is dangerous to trifle with a cross Punimin. Some learn that the easy way. Some the hard.

The farming village Pistol Rose's family shares with several other tribes is nestled in a beautiful haven of woods. They live off the land and carry on as carpenters and tradespeople, tanners, smiths, hunters, and gardeners. Most of their homemade gadgetry, whether created here or stolen from Strelkie and augmented, supports farming, work, feeding and the like. Their spindly contraptions of wood and metal at once seem to threaten the laws of physics and please them.

Punimin constantly work, tinker, and craft things. Artisans in their own right. Most families are mixes of races (some by choice and some by the way the cards land on birthing days), and each family has a unique style of dress to distinguish itself from its friendly neighbors. You'll never mistake a Clock for a Teeth or a Pistol for a Firelock.

Their surnames come first, and have something to do with the families' dominant proficiency—though the brand of a name doesn't always predict expertise or even accurate function on an individual basis. Surprises and disappointments are part of life here. Expectations are tentatively welcome but have been known to yield dangerous fruit in even the kindest of families. Only a village's holy man may add a word before his surname, and this word is always Elderman. No one else is allowed a distinguishing marker such as that.

Rose hurries along with a shaggy dog, back from her rendezvous with Lilly. Suddenly, Clock Dancin, a boy of around twelve, tackles her and pins her with a rough-hewn fighting stick. Unlike most boys, he doesn't have a lot of stories and boasts carved on his stick. The only thing on his rod is a single crude rendering of Rose.

"Yield, Pistol!" he shouts.

"Clock Dancin, you stupid boy!" She head-fakes, then smashes the stick against his forehead and knocks him off.

He chuckles. "That was great. Teach me that?"

She moves him onto the grassy ground and gets on top of him with another stick. Puts his hands where they go. She tells him, "Head-fake so they lean back."

He slowly butts his head toward her.

She slowly leans back. "Now I'm off balance. You feel that? Now shove up."

He shoves the stick gently and it touches her forehead. It's a delicate moment. He's in love.

She doesn't know. "When it's a Strelkie soldier, aim for under the nose so the bone smashes up into their brain. You can also knee them in the groin and mash their tender bits."

"Yeah. Okay." He looks nervous.

She gently knee-taps him between his legs and climbs off. He moans like it hurts. She chuckles, "Whatever, cud." She drags him to his feet. He's fine.

He walks with her. "Did your mom let you work on the Line at the border hospital finally?"

Rose glares at him. "No, I was with you all day." He looks confused because she wasn't. She adds, "Dancin. I was with you. All day."

"Oh, yeah, I remember." He grins. "I think you kissed me, right?"

She smacks his stomach hard with the stick.

He loses his wind and chokes. "My mistake. It's all clear, haha! Hey, guess what? Your cousin Ann is getting married. Just proposed."

"Whoa! That's great!" Rose is overjoyed. She can hardly believe the good news and has to remind herself to breathe. Cousin Ann is Rose's closest friend in the whole family, her fiercest ally, and who Rose wants to be when she gets older—though Ann doesn't know any of this. Ann has so long been concerned with the frustrating matters of boys that her attention has lingered away from the family.

But Rose admires everything about Ann. Rose is a quiet study of her, and a locktrap of conversations and memories about her as far back as she can remember. Winning Ann's approval over a knife hilt well-carved, or a joke well-timed, though rare, is everything to Rose. Ann would never give Rose advice (except perhaps to not follow other people's advice, or to avoid the ratty boys and the lying boys and the cheating boys), but Rose takes advice from Ann in every way she can gather, through careful observation, from how she models her hair, to how she smiles when she's having devilishly clever thoughts, to how she carries weapons in ways that show them off but without looking like she's trying to show them off. And with this unexpected news of Ann's pending marriage, Rose suddenly realizes that the impossible isn't so impossible after all. For Ann has now, after years of fretting and sorting and fighting and believing, finally done what everyone said would never happen: she found a man who meets her high basic standards, and who will change his name to Pistol so that her many forthcoming babies will champion the family name further into history. Somehow, impossible-to-please Ann found her soulmate. Rose admires her even more for staying her course and refusing to abandon her dream.

One day, Ann will admire Rose back.

Rose shakes herself out of her thoughts and drags Dancin by the arm to come with her. They run together.

"Can I make you a clock?" Dancin asks her.

"Why?" Rose asks.

"Because I'm getting good at it, and your family doesn't have any clocks. You're the only Punimin who don't, I think. Most Punimin keep a whole variety."

"Maybe we're just not interested."

Dancin struggles to keep apace with her. "Rose, you can't not be interested. The East Range Punimin keep clocks, the Wood Dunes Punimin keep clocks, the Southern Peninsula Punimin have the most clocks, and this entire wilderness of people, except for you Pistols, have clocks. It's the best way to keep carved records and stories."

"We carve our stories on the walls of our house just like everybody else. Clocks are redundant, Dancin."

"But you can't take your house to visit its stories onto a cousin across the continent. Clocks travel."

Rose stops and looks him in the eyes, regretfully sharing harsh news. "Clocks are fragile. They break. That isn't the Pistol way."

He frowns. "But some clocks are incredibly resilient. Some are carved out of logs or stone, or assembled from reclaimed steamships, or twirled out of tough nature like birds' nests with the screws and gears of engineering hidden under decorative growings like pleasant cyborg cobblings."

"Uh-huh."

"My grandfather made a clock as tall as me out of stone. It's sculpted with legendary family history."

"I've seen it. He carved himself and your grandma naked, in their prime, with impressively grand physiques." She smiles, teasing. "What a tale."

Dancin turns flush. "Don't argue with recorded history, Rose," he whispers, afraid of being overheard. "That's how people wind up sculpted into the next album of clocks with diabolically unflattering details."

"Clocks shouldn't keep more than time," she says. "And you're wrong, Dancin. My family *does* have a clock." She walks on and Dancin keeps up with her.

"I haven't seen it," he says.

"It's in the attic. Or maybe the shed. The Irons gave it to us.

It's a tree stump carved into an owl. Or it might be a falcon. We're not really sure; it's not very good."

"I think I should make your family a proper clock. I'll put our friendship on it, as a history."

"Clock Dancin, you're the only clock I care to keep."

He grins at her as they bound along. He won't stop smiling, until she punches him in the shoulder. But that just makes him laugh, which makes her smile.

They stop short.

The local Punimin gather around a Strelkie magistrate nailing up a NOTICE in the center of their village by the main well. This place is not as large as a town square, but if there's a dance or a village meal, this is where it happens, on the packed dirt. There aren't columns like in the city, nor is there an executioner's stage, but there are towering celebration posts with familial carvings all up and down them. Outside of their elderman's church, it's the most sacred place in the village. And this Strelkie intruder is like a fly in an oil painting, come to scratch and ruin everything it can.

The threat of war lingers over everyone anyway, Punimin and Strelkie alike, as a sticky wind because the tools of war are all around and celebrated. Moments like this make it all the more likely. Strelkie and Punimin love weapons, both ceremonial and sharp. Strelkie citizens tend to think of knives and axes and guns as more like belt buckles or earrings, something to be noticed at a party, and unless it's a soldier's, the weapon is almost always ceremonial. Of course, for many Strelkie, ceremonies are an agnostic affair, and like their holidays, go largely unobserved. Punimin enjoy much more meaning in their weapons. Punimin children are taught to make their own as toys from the very beginning. Crossbow slingshots and wooden guns are particular favorites.

Ornamentation on this hilt or that curve is decorative and flashy, and pride is taken in how impressive the work is, and it all comes from a real experience like a hunt or a fight or an achievement. Even a carving of a first kiss could wind up on an axe head or sling handle. And these prided tools are as recognizable as the faces hammered onto them: Punimin families invent their own unique symbols with their own meanings; nothing is faked or forgotten. Old fights are fondly remembered, and fresh fights are sometimes coveted. So every hammering hit of the nail that Strelkie magistrate smashes to affix her NOTICE to this Punimin village center edges peoples' fingers closer to those weapons. Closer to earning new marks. Some Punimin don't even realize they're doing it. But that invading hammer, that violent graffiti of kingspeak, is an irresistible call to arms. The Strelkie soldiers charged with protecting the magistrate, however, absolutely notice those unconscious reaching fingers and hands.

An argument suddenly breaks out between the nervous Strelkie magistrate who doesn't want to be here, her small contingent of Strelkie soldiers who look ready for a fight, and the large mass of outraged Punimin who look well-past reasoning. Rose and Dancin watch the grownups froth-shout.

Rose learns through Dancin's excellent long-distance spying glass that this NOTICE is the unthinkable result of some recently resolved Strelkie matters: King Harrol's decades-long foreign enemy, the Pirate Sisters, a landless army of ruthless plunderers, has just unexpectedly surrendered in their faraway war over some string of islands or "water colonies" that most Punimin have never heard of. Harrol has claimed his vanquished opponent's vast wealth, or so goes the news, and his army is now sailing home.

Fragments of arguments Rose overhears add to the news:

Harrol doesn't want his war soldiers to live in his peaceful, utopian city. His warriors have a reputation for being ... less than civilized. They don't respect soft citizens, utopian ideas, patience, kindness, virgins, or anything that tells them "No." They're used to fighting for what they want and getting it, no matter the cost. In them, Harrol has made wild beasts without collars. They need land.

It is widely whispered that the king fears his own army but wants them close by, near the city where they can be managed and called upon easily. So he is deciding, via this NOTICE, to make them live in the wilderness with the Punimin here, rather than sending them to Fort Mary in the Punimin ranges (too crowded already), or Fort Favor by the Death Coast against the Punimin wood dunes (too far), or Fort Ethe east of the Punimin wilderness (there is a longstanding treaty with the neighboring Kingdom of Barbellics to keep that fort staffed with a low number). The "open wilderness" is the only place the king can stick his people. And so, it shall be.

This new arrangement does not find the Punimin who live here waving open arms.

Strelkie soldiers tussle with a feisty grandma, Iron Ruthie, who gets knocked down. She flails and becomes tangled in her dress, an apron stocked with odd, crooked hand tools and hammers. Punimin help her back up, but she doesn't need the assistance.

The magistrate nervously yells, "You're lucky we don't kill your entire village for this disrespect!"

Iron Ruthie isn't scared of anything. "We could tear you to pieces quicker than your mothers knew your fathers! *You're* lucky! You godless mules." Ruthie doesn't realize she's pulled a throwing hammer from her hip. But the outnumbered soldiers do.

A Strelkie soldier shoots a gun at Ruthie's feet—she hesitates, then spreads her arms to stop her group from retaliating. "No. They're baiting you." She knows the Punimin here easily have these soldiers by the numbers, but the soldiers brought enough gunpowder weapons to tilt the scales in their favor. Even the most practiced general couldn't predict who would win and who would be ashes by morning. Rose catches herself clutching two rocks to throw the moment people start fighting. She's ready.

Truly, war is ripe on the tree and the gentlest gust could bring a fall no one is quite ready for. It would be an avalanche in both directions, and they all know it. Enough of them want it that the wiser folks hold their breath. Or maybe they aren't the wiser folks.

Two squirrels start fighting and shouting on a nearby tree and draw everyone's attention. The little varmints tussle on the bark, and one throws the other off the trunk. They skitter across the dirt and chase through the legs of the assembled mob and soldiers as if they aren't even there, and sprint away chattering curses into the brush to an unknowable fate. The interruption cools the crowd just enough that the Strelkie soldiers are able to escort the magistrate away from the boiling Punimin mob before anyone can regain their angry momentum.

Rose and Dancin approach to read the fine print at the bottom of the NOTICE, and learn the worst part yet: to maintain order, the king is now decreeing more Strelkie laws will be *strictly enforced* on the Punimin, across the whole continent, starting right here. This has never been done before. The Punimin have enjoyed full memories of being shunned and largely ignored by His Majesty. But now the returning Strelkie soldiers will be the police to enforce King's Law. It is a vile plan by the king to keep his wild and bloodthirsty warlords busy, so they won't turn on him. He's adding wood to the far side of a fire with nothing but a futile wish to keep it from driving toward him.

The Punimin do not take this news well.

"We should go into the city and cut the king's throat!" Rose's father, Pistol David, bellows as he stabs a knife into the kitchen table in their cottage home. He absently scratches the old skull brand on his hand, though it doesn't ever itch. Grace can always tell how hot her husband David's rage is because that scratching is like a steam release valve. She never comments on this tick of his, for worry that he would stop doing it and take away her advantage of being able to read a small piece of his mind. As for her, she hides her skull brand scar with a bracelet that dangles beads, or a leather hunting glove that her grandfather made, or a wrist scarf. She hates the Strelkie for marring Punimin for life with these brands. The children care about these marks less—it's just the way of things, and has been since the practice was instituted by Ward Harrol sometime during the Greatest War, over one-hundred years ago, for mixed reasons that no one can agree on. It doesn't seem to become an emotional issue for most Punimin until later in adulthood, as the good scars earned through living and fighting and learning build up on their arms and legs, and they realize that this skull brand is the one carving they didn't choose—and the one about which no tall tale can adjust into a better story. It's a cow tag. A bullet wound is better, because how one came to acquire *that* can change depending on the listener ... and how many hints or hollers of alcohol the wound-bearer has had at the time of the telling.

As Rose's family argues about how badly the king needs to die, her gaze drifts around her home, like it might while listening to traveling home musicians. War-talk and music feel the same to her, inspiring. This cottage is more of a worn shack, a narrow two-story log cabin. You can tell the history of a family by their home: simple drawings and carvings line every wall from the floor to the windowsills—these are places where the youngest children are allowed to tell stories. The war-talk almost animates these scrawled stories in Rose's mind. From the windowsills to the top door hinges, the growing children practice their drawing and chiseling, chronicling holidays and wonderful times. The elders take the tops of the walls, where the craftsmanship generally shines and tells older stories from their youth. But nothing is so significant as the ceilings—simple wooden beams are found painted and chiseled with great stories of battling beasts like giant walrus-tigers, lore from the Fourth Age, and fantasies about overthrowing the king in battle one day. But no family ever carves their own ceiling —that space is reserved for honored guests who live outside the home. It is uncommon to visit a Punimin friend without leaving your mark on their home, and if your story at dinner is well-received, you will be asked to add it to their ceiling—with colors—before the end of breakfast. This practice keeps families remembering that there are infinitely more happenings going on in the world outside of their homes than inside. It keeps their children dreaming when they look up at the ceiling out of bed at night. And it makes otherwise simple cabins intense pieces of layered art and history.

Pistol David worries that all this history will be destroyed. "King's Law is a creeping thing," he warns. "It pushes down whatever's in front of it. We could lose our homes."

"No one is saying that," Grace tries to ease him. "The edict isn't about that." She has a copy of the edict in her hands, already well-read and worn. She's trying not to tremble, but the edges of the parchment shake just a little and give away her nerves.

"The edict *is* about that, if you read it right," Madrick insists. "Strelkie don't keep history. They'll burn our houses down."

Rose fears what would happen to her people if they lost their homes and the stories carved into them. The quality of the art in these homes may vary—not everyone is expert at rendering a quick sculpture on a ceiling beam or doorframe, and rickety ladders are often blamed for affecting a storyteller's ability to detail properly, but some people are quite expert indeed, and sharing each new added marvel keeps neighbors visiting neighbors. Punimin can hardly be stopped from dragging knives over any piece of wood that comes near them. When a child breaks an arm, the splint is always made of wood simply so it can be carved and saved. Church pews are known to have fresh wood chippings after every service. The Punimin whittle and mark; that is just their way. Every building or house is like a clock in that regard—a careful record-keeping, tall-tale-boasting, history-checking, breathing machine of story and life. *Keep your blade sharp, your wood cut, and your stories coming.*

As talk turns to using guns against the king, Rose looks to the center of this Pistol house, where stands the hearth, of course, but the chimney is uniquely built out of melted guns instead of stones. Pistols never throw broken guns away; they simply retire them into construction. And, should an intruder ever be so bold and stupid as to visit a Pistol's house with malintent, they might find that a surprising number of old guns smashed into the walls are significantly less retired than advertised.

Rose's thoughts drift back to dinner and the present as her family's argument suddenly gets louder. The kitchen is crowded with more than iron pots and wooden plates. The whole Pistol family is here: Rose, her father Pistol David, mother Pistol Grace, younger sister Pistol Jennifer, uncle Pistol Madrick, and cousins Pistol Beau and dear Pistol Ann, Madrick's children. How I miss some of them now.

David finishes reading the edict for the twelfth time. It makes him madder every time his eyes cut across the words. "This is impossible to follow. It contradicts itself. We should slice the king's throat. Slow. The Strelkie love public executions, right?" David hits the table loudly. "This edict squeezes King's Law more tightly around our throats than ever before. It's an axe dangling over our heads. They should've written this on chains, not parchment."

"David." Grace whispers like a bite. "Please settle down." The "please" is for his benefit, a warning.

He misses it. "We can't follow King's Law, Grace! This is too far! Now marriage is *illegal?!* They could enforce this on us. The Strelkie are barbarians! Worse than the Wolf people of the Southern Fire Straits."

Rose's cousin Ann speaks up. "I can still get married—"

Rose perks up at that, but Uncle Madrick raps loudly on the table and angrily snatches the edict. The fancy parchment that cost more than his boots upsets him almost as much as the words so elegantly scrawled on the damn thing. "'Family units are a threat to Unity. The purpose of *rotating* children, sexual partners, and *property* is to create one unified society.' They can unify my ass."

David is beside himself. "Insane. You know, I heard every Strelkie uses drugs to cope? Drugs! I'll bet it's that frog powder. Probably came from the Chemical People."

Cousin Ann tries to be heard a second time. "I can still get married—"

"How?" Rose asks.

Ann's father Madrick cuts them off. "The Strelkie are idiots! How can their god-king be alive? He won The Greatest War one hundred and twelve years ago when he was forty-five!"

Madrick's son Beau takes the edict from him. "They have advanced medicine. That's how. Maybe living more like Strelkie is worth trying. We can't stop them—"

David counters, "Yes, let's surrender our freedom to live like useless quisbis who do nothing for ourselves."

Beau argues, "Ward Harrol does provide for them. They don't have to work so hard or struggle like we do. We sleep on boards and straw. I hear they sleep on something like clouds."

"Probably do. Their backs are caved and weak," Madrick grumbles.

"If I could say something about marriage?" Ann asks.

Rose points at Ann to second the topic like a nomination, but this is ignored.

"Our heaviest burdens are simple tricks for the Strelkie," Beau insists. "The king has it so streamlined he gives *every citizen* technology like we've never seen. Gifts just for following King's Law. They have good clocks—every Strelkie home has the same clock over a cold marble mantle: a holographic globe of the world depicting the Four Known Continents, with the clock hands pivoting from a marked point in the Beast Sea where the equator and prime meridian intersect. Inside this globe smiles a life-sized digital head of the king. It's said to be amazing."

"Amazing?" David asks. "Like the earth is a helmet and the king the source of its life? Yes, that sounds truly amazing. All this flattering magnificence to His Majesty must make the telling of time difficult."

"Especially when you can tell time by the sun, if you know anything," Madrick grumbles.

"Do you think the Strelkie hate their clocks but just keep them to act like they love the king?" little Jennifer asks.

Rose nods big as she bites into a bread roll. "Yep. Kiss-asses," Rose says through the bread—but too loudly, because her mother Grace whaps the back of her head with a wooden spoon. Rose's chewed bread flies out of her mouth and plops onto the center of the table, making a silly little "splat" sound, and Rose laughs with Jennifer about it.

Ann briefly half-smiles at Rose, who immediately begins wondering if she can create another splat and win that half-smile again.

But Ann wouldn't notice if she did. "I have to say something about marriage," Ann says more firmly than before.

"Hold on, Ann," Beau says. "Let me finish. None of you understand my point. This change that's happening, it may not be the end of the world. We don't have to see it that way. The Strelkie way of doing things—they live well, better than we can even dream."

Rose's mother says pointedly, "Beau, their Definitive History, which it sounds like you've somehow read, has no place in your mind. Strelkie think everyone who's not Strelkie is a pack of thieves without the slightest wisdom behind their eyes. This is the way of all rulers in all the Four Known Continents of the world."

"None of us truly know about the rest of the world beyond our own continent," Beau argues, "except for words repeated by those who claim to have met pirates."

"I've met pirates," Madrick says.

Beau rolls his eyes. "Fishermen."

"No, *pirates*," Madrick insists.

"Beau," Grace says, "these rumors you've heard about how wonderful the Strelkie are, they're lies—"

"I don't think so," Beau says.

"I'll prove it," Grace retorts. "You know that much of what you think about these people is assumption. Yes?"

Beau doesn't want to nod but he does a little.

Grace continues, "And assumptions have a sneaky way of becoming facts, which is just another word for lies when your neighbor has a different set of them. This makes knowledge itself the reserved and preferred business of 'leaders,' but it is all really just a knuckled barrel of guesses that they sell as truths and dreams and *chains* around your neck. Dress it up however you like, Beau, but Strelkie people are servants."

Beau shakes his head. "They're not, Aunt Grace; machines do everything for the Strelkie. Servants don't control the temperature indoors. Or fly in balloons. Or talk to each other from miles apart—"

Madrick is a burly man with a big mouth, so when he speaks gently, the family pays closer attention. "Strelkie don't live miles apart, son. They're stacked together in that city. Those are flowery carver lies. You should know better."

"We're not that different," Beau says. "Both of our peoples like anachronistic machines—"

"The Strelkie would never outfit a shovel into a steam powered jiggler to make it smartly vibrate when it digs," Grace says. "They aren't thinking people. We love marrying technologies out of place as much as we enjoy good matchmaking in love. 'The more wild, the more fruitful.' Strelkie enjoy nothing."

"Speaking of marrying ..." Ann whispers, gritting her teeth.

Rose is caught up in the argument and wants to contribute, so she says, "Strelkie really don't enjoy anything. They have unnecessary wooden gloves with gears to hold things away from their hands. I heard."

"Who'd you hear that from?" David asks.

"Uh, a Clock boy," Rose lies.

"You and your clock boy. What do Clocks know?" David asks.

Ann pats on Rose's hand to stay quiet, and Rose stills herself with a silence that she hopes Ann notices.

Madrick gets angrier as he talks, "That city is littered with offbeat, useless tools that the people think are in vogue but they're not. You don't see a stick of litter here, Beau. Not a stick. Don't defend those monsters. Don't be fooled by their flashy false promises. They're backwards! They outlaw marriage! Assassination is the discussion we should be having instead of your culture envy or whatever this is."

Pistol Ann pounds the table. "I can still get married! There is a provision!" She snatches the edict.

Rose grins at Ann's ferocious might.

Ann isn't upset that they didn't let her speak—she knows a Pistol has to fight for what she wants, and she blames herself for being meek. She blames the fresh intoxication of romance she's found for softening her normally edged spit. No one is shocked at her outburst; in fact, they respect it. Until she continues with, "You just need consent from the district emissary. It's a fee, and permission. I can win favor."

This confuses Rose. Ann isn't one to ask for permission; permission is too akin to advice. But Ann has always been sneakily clever, so maybe there is something to this method?

Beau grumbles, "You're lucky, sis. Strelkie wouldn't even let *me* ask. Maybe one day, if our cultures successfully merge. Which will never happen if we assassinate the king—"

Now it's Beau's turn to get left behind as Rose's father warns Ann, "Asking for permission means they can say no."

"Aye," Madrick agrees. "Babies learn 'no' before 'yes.' And Strelkie? Strelkie stay babies."

Rose's mother Grace tries to bring what she would call sanity to this discussion. "Getting married without permission is treason now. If a Strelkie breaks a law, they kill two innocent citizen friends and maim five more. What would they do to us?"

Madrick grins a war-smile. "Bounce off, like rain on stone."

Grace has little patience for her brother-in-law. "Their soldiers have never lost a battle in all the histories, Madrick."

Madrick doesn't look so sure of that. "I can tell stories, too, Grace." He tosses a double-barreled revolver onto the table: the bone handle has a carving of Madrick surfing on the backs of two oxen. "Bad histories carve easy."

Ann urges them, "What would the Strelkie gain from hurting us? This edict says the district emissary only disallows a Punimin marriage in 'extreme circumstances.' What could that even be? There's no reason not to ask permission."

David grouses, "I can't believe this is happening. Three

hundred and forty-seven years into the Fifth Age, and now we're under the thumb of ignorant tyrannical barbarians in golden towers who know nothing about real people."

Ann says, "It doesn't matter what they know. *We* know something: to get along with them or pay the price."

"Is that you talking, or your planned husband?" Madrick asks.

Ann says, "This king, the next king, or three kings from now —this is just how it is. We can fight a lot of people; we can't fight the world. *But they will respect our asking.* All the Strelkie want is respect. Cooperation. We'll show it, and we'll get permission. Then they'll leave us alone—and that's the whole point."

Rose speaks up. "I think you should get married in secret."

"In secret? How? There are no secrets the king does not know," Ann argues.

Rose feels a deep stab of pain for Ann cutting at her like that.

Ann says, "The Pirate Sisters believed in all that sprawhammid nonsense and look where it got them—butchered on their own seas."

David grumbles, "Butchered? Mmm. I doubt that one."

"What's sprawhammid?" Rose asks.

Madrick answers, "It's an old word, means thinking for yourself."

Grace argues, "No, it means adventuring against the tide. Just a silly pirate saying for fools who end up drowned or beheaded or worse."

Beau mutters, "I read 'sprawhammid' used to mean more than that—"

"Well, I'm no pirate," Ann says. "But I am a Pistol, and that's supposed to mean I'm clever. I don't keep secrets or risk meaningless adventures for no good reason like a fool. I want to keep my head and my husband-to-be's head right where they are. Strelkie permission is the fastest, easiest, smartest road to my marriage. It's how I get what I want from our enemies. They will give me permission."

Rose admires Ann's fierceness, but she shakes her head. Still stung by Ann cutting at her before, she cuts back, though a little softer. Rose says, "I'd do it in secret. Don't trust the Strelkie. They worship an old man as a god. That's not too smart."

Ann snaps back, "Oh, what do you know about Strelkie, Rose? You'd pee yourself if you ever saw one up close. You can draw whatever you want on your play knives, but you don't know real battle."

Rose hides the nearly tear-inducing effect of Ann's snap with a forced shrug of feigned ambivalence. Rose's secrets are her own.

Ann looks to Madrick and asks, "Dad?"

Madrick has always been tough on Ann, to build her up to be strong and confident. She looks so much like her mother did at that age, and Madrick often questions himself about whether he should be so tough. He wants Ann to be better than his wife was. He wonders if that pressure is a mistake—if it's having the opposite effect. When Ann looks into his eyes, she sees him weighing scales of judgment. A heavy sigh from him could break her in this moment. But she can't possibly know that he isn't judging her— he's judging himself. He wants to be a better father but doesn't know how. He wishes he knew what future this decision would bring, but he doesn't. Regardless of the consequences, he knows this needs to be her choice, not his. His uncharacteristically soft smile means to say all of that, but it would take a voice he won't lend for her to actually hear it. He holds her firmly by the hand with his usual iron grip and says, as kindly as he can, "I share my brother's mind on this. I think it's a mistake. But it's your decision, Ann. You have to make it."

Ann lets a single tear fall and turns to Rose. It's the first time Ann has ever seemed to ask Rose for advice, and she does it without a word.

"Do it in secret," Rose whispers.

Ann doesn't seem content with that advice, because she briskly excuses herself from the table and goes outside.

Rose wonders if it would be better to side with Ann and support her idea to wrench permission from the Strelkie. But as much as Rose wants Ann to like her, Rose isn't capable of saying something she doesn't believe. Not when it's this serious. At the age of ten, she's just too stubborn to do that.

CHAPTER III
ANN'S SONG

As if to outdo their shared obsession with gizmos, in both Strelkie and Punimin cultures there is a ubiquity of bold clothing that refuses to go out of style between generations; extreme and colorful designs, an everlasting steampunk aesthetic, that permeates the richest elite's dinner garments and the bog cleaner's hat and spectacles. Everything is a marriage of old and new. No matter their struggles or their pains or their torments, Strelkie and Punimin all take care to look exactly as they wish to. But none take so much care to look outstanding as Strelkie in the middle of the ladder of power, who wish to climb. And none are more center-burdened than district emissaries. Oh, those dreadful people.

The Strelkie have such a district emissary assigned in a plain, freshly built log cabin office at one corner of this Punimin village. The Punimin feel like it's a guard tower, though it's only one story. It is an outpost placed as a "diplomatic outreach," but has swiftly become more of a "spying post" due to the attempts at outreach being met with bitten fingers. All the carvings on this structure are on the outside; none are on the inside (Strelkie do not redesign anything; all that comes from the king is good as-is, hear hear) and these outside carvings are of the unflattering, graffiti variety. Judging from the stories told on the walls of the building, the Punimin believe the Strelkie are obsessed with an impressive variety of vile, carnal acts that are unsuitable to be viewed by children—though children are as likely to carve such stories here as adults, because a child bravely sneaking a carving onto Strelkie property and getting away with it isn't just a game, it's a rite of passage and a clear path to respect. The crasser and more creative the carving, the more critical praise from one's peers a child can earn. To say that a vast group of adults don't play a version of the same competitive game well into their nineties would be a lie—they're just quieter about it.

The Pistol family, and Pistol Ann's groom-to-be, a big strong fellow named Forge Hoss, enter the enemy's cabin and stand humbly before an overly polished and overly hatted Strelkie emissary in his stuffy wooden office. Ann and Hoss wear gloves over their skull brands to look more "presentable" to the Strelkie from whom they have permission to ask. Beau keeps his hands in his pockets, David rubs his brand nervously, Grace wears her beaded watch, and the rest don't give their brand a thought at all.

The walls are plain, but an air-cooling machine made of birchwood and bronze vibrates in a window and blows air so hard that it rattles the ornamental pistol bullets on Beau's vest. He holds out his hand and enjoys the cold air. Madrick gently smacks his hand down—they're not here to enjoy Strelkie amenities. Madrick is wearing a vest of heavy knives, and thick pants with three guns strapped to each leg. The mechanical breeze does not stir him in any way. He sweats defiantly. And the skull brand on his hand isn't something he hides or shies away from—especially not here among the Strelkie. He grips his collar to make sure the back of his hand shows outward so that all can see his mark. Madrick is the one who always holds his hand so the skull brand can be seen. He calls it Punimin pride, but really it's a chip on his shoulder and a dare for anyone to confront him. He knows he would have been better off born into times of open war, where he could put his hands to use on a battlefield breaking bones. He used to think of venturing south into the Fire Straits as a boy just to look for trouble, or to band with a group of glorious legends like The Dead Assassins—whom he believes exist despite the naysayers—or to seek out the Chemical People for some real trouble, but then he had children and turned fully to rearing them. These times of slowly eroding peace and creeping abuse torture him because, if war *is* coming to his people, he'd like to face it while he's still in his prime. He hopes that if a Strelkie scoffs at the skull brand on his hand, maybe he can get something started—a fight or a kill that sparks his people to act. But so far no one has ever taken his bait, or cared. He doesn't mean as much to the Strelkie as they mean to him, and that makes him all the more mad.

The glossily dressed emissary, a pudgy little man with peachy cheeks named Galley Waith, counts a stack of coins the Pistols brought and reviews their submitted documents at a round desk made of painstakingly blown glass with colorful crystals inside. The desk is meant to display power and beauty, its shimmering bits are probably booty from some far-off conquered so-and-so, but it's only good for catching dust and blinding people when the sun strikes it. Waith is a sneery gentleman who leaves fingerprints all over this desk and believes his station in life ought to be in the city, not out here in the "brush." He observes from under his tall hat, "You have the proper fee, and your medical documents are in order."

Smiles flit across the Pistol family, but Rose and Madrick remain skeptical and guarded. Madrick flexes his branded hand.

"Groom, step forward," Emissary Waith says. The groom Forge Hoss obliges, and Waith orders, "Drop your pants and present."

No one looks like they heard that right. Forge Hoss mutters, "I'm sorry?"

Patience is a robe Emissary Waith does not wear. "Guard!"

A smarmy Strelkie soldier stomps in with an oversized gun with steaming pipes and gears. It looks like it shoots arrow spikes. Waith continues, "Drop your pants and present. It's part of the application—I don't like it either, believe me. Come on. Quickly, lad; I have other business today."

A second, viperish Strelkie soldier strolls in with a whip spiked all along its woven thong with shark teeth. Pistol Grace turns her daughters Jennifer and Rose away to offer the groom some privacy. Forge Hoss drops his pants.

Emissary Waith is disinterested but scratches down the required note. "And back up." Waith writes *another* note as Ann's groom-to-be hitches up his pants. Waith says dryly, "Despite being defectively big for normal applications, the king now wants more sizable men for future wars. The groom is hereby drafted into the city stalls to provide less desirable Strelkie women with large offspring—for the rest of his life. This marriage is disallowed."

Ann screams, "What?!" The blood seems to instantly flee her cheeks.

"You can't do that!" Forge Hoss shouts. He doesn't know if

his heart is beating too quickly or stopped all together. He quivers like an electric fever has him. His body is in shock, not working and only just managing to stay standing. He's in a choking panic.

Before Rose can even fantasize about how she might kill Waith in some way that she could get away with it, the soldiers bash Forge Hoss over the head so badly with a club that he bleeds onto the glass desk and falls unconscious. They drag the groom-now-never-to-be out of the room and away *forever*. Pistol David holds his niece Ann back, but Ann's father Madrick steps forward to bring a physical solution to a paper problem—

Waith points a gun at him. "Are you attempting to break *King's Law?* Your district emissary has ruled. I gave you animals more grace than you deserve by allowing you to enter this property with your silly family weapons that make you feel safe. I did that for your dignity. Clearly, I was too kind. Leave now, before I remember your family name."

Rose notices that Waith's belt has the old style of being a bandolier with many nooks for bullets. But he doesn't carry bullets. Those are finger bones. And names are written on each sheath.

Madrick must notice too—he is willing to lose a few digits, but he won't risk a hair on Ann's head. So he bites his tongue to the point that a little blood drips out, and he lets Ann weep in his arms. Rose's mother Grace gets everyone out of there quickly and quietly, like a mother hen who just witnessed a fox tear a chick from them and she wants no chance for additional torments.

The Pistol family shuffles away from Emissary Waith's cabin, defeated and confused—except for Rose. She *knew* what would happen. Several Strelkie soldiers follow them like instigating wolves, actually howling, and hoping for a fight. Madrick breathes loudly in an attempt to drive his ears deaf, but he can't drown out those instigating howlers. He makes up a tune and hums it. It's a brooding anthem.

A traveling man with long whiskers happens to be nearby and hears it, a man only slightly younger than Madrick. He's wearing robes indicating his pupilship in studying to become an elderman. He lets Madrick's pained song stick into his ears, and he walks away meditating on it. He reproduces it himself with a whistle, and he adjusts it, tinkers its tune, and changes it into a more upbeat and catchy song. That long-whiskered man will carry that melody for the rest of his days, wherever he goes, and the people who encounter him will seldom forget him, or his song, and they won't know why. His pleasantly whistled song, turned from Madrick's pain, will scarcely leave the listener's minds for years.

Grace herds her brood. "Move along. Keep walking. Don't even look at them. We're going straight home."

Her husband David looks back at the Strelkie soldiers with hate. They seem to be all over the place, "occupying" this corner of the village. Some of them start to pull down the wooden celebration posts in the center of town to use as a fence line around the emissary's cabin. They think it will keep the Punimin from carving the cabin's walls. Really a fence will just add more meat to the bone for them to chew on. David is already imagining the marks he's going to make.

Grace whispers to David, "Please." But she means to say, "You'll be sorry when we get home if you don't listen to me and leave now." He hears all of that unsaid warning and obeys. He's only in charge of this family because, and when, she says so. They all walk on. Madrick has to carry Ann. Between his heavy humming and Ann's need to be held, he manages to walk in the safe direction. But it feels like a retreat, and he doesn't like it one bit.

Rose is shaken to see her hero Ann be completely broken in this way. A small part of Rose almost hates Ann for it, and she's never felt that way toward Ann before. Rose glances back at one of the Strelkie soldiers, who laughs at her. He waves at her to come to him and holds out a pretty watch. She imagines what that watch would look like stuck sideways in his throat—and she could make that happen, right now—but she doesn't take the bait.

That night, when Rose goes to fetch her parents who disappeared minutes before dinner, she finds them sitting together in their bedroom. She spies on them from the cracked door. Their bed has four posts, and they're taking a few minutes together to carve on one of them. Rose can't see the stories they've embedded on these posts, and she never goes into their room, but this stolen moment strikes her. Even with all the chaos of the day, they've taken three minutes to themselves while dinner cools. There is certainly a sadness hanging over them for Ann, but as they whittle together, there's a calmness, and a firm, resilient happiness that belongs only to them. Rose wonders what that's like. She doesn't know why, but this moment sticks in her mind forever and much more clearly than the other event of the night that would come shortly. She gently raps on the door and tells them the meat has cooled enough to eat.

The Pistol family slowly consumes a pig dinner in silence. Ann isn't here. Rose quietly teaches her little sister Jennifer how to block sword moves with their forks under the table, at their knees. Rose pins Jennifer's hand, and Jennifer comes up with a small wooden toy gun and shoots Rose with two acorn bullets that bounce off but sting. Rose nods her approval: never shoot an enemy only once if you can afford more shots.

Her father David breaks the quiet. "We should fight them. Now."

Grace won't have it. "War costs life on both sides, David. You know the true histories. It's both sides who lose—no matter who tells the tale in the end—it's always both sides."

"Then there's only one thing we can do," he says. "Leave. I've traded letters with people who moved to Afar."

Beau perks up. "The Jungle Country? Is it real?"

"No. They're salesmen after money and jewels," Grace says. "David's been sending letters all over the world since he was a boy."

Her husband disagrees. "And sometimes I hear back. I think Afar is a real place."

"Named 'Afar.' Mm-hmm. Salesmen." Grace thinks she has ended this idea.

But David isn't finished. "It's beyond the Beast Sea. That's past Ward Harrol's reach. Uncharted."

Grace shakes her head. "It's more dangerous to cross the sea than it is to stay here, David. That's why they have to send letters by bird. Boats and men fail those Pirate Sister waters more than the stories even tell."

"At least they're free of Strelkie in Afar." David is desperate. "They don't have to worship Ward Harrol, as we're likely to be made to do. Next the church will be barred. You'll see. And that swamp keeping the Punimin out on the peninsulas away from all of this won't hold back the Strelkie forever. This entire continent will be hell under that damn king. Everything good he touches turns to ash. But the jungle ... Strelkie won't cross the Beast Sea. We can do it."

Little Jennifer is excited. She's not even seven yet. "I want to live in a free jungle! Weren't our ancestors adventurers? It's in our blood. I know I'm adopted, but I still get the same ancestors, right?"

David pleads with his wife, "Let me write my friends in Afar again and ask if we can go. How long until King's Law changes and says we can't stay married? I'm being serious. Will they split us apart to scrub their buildings and oil their machines? Do you think Strelkie City is the only city they'll ever build? Will our daughters become forced labor like Punimin past? Worse? And what of our grandchildren one day—if our children are even allowed to keep children at all by then—"

Grace gives him a look that shuts him down. "I think it would be better if Ann joined us for supper. She has studied everything there is to know about the appeals process. We should talk about the things in front of us, not grind our wheels on roads that aren't made yet. Madrick, get Ann?"

Madrick looks lost in grief. He didn't hear her; he's just carving the emissary's face into a pistol handle. He's so quiet that Rose almost forgot he was sitting here. She says, "I'll go get her, Uncle Madrick." She excuses herself from the table and leaps away with soft footsteps.

Upstairs in an attic-like corner of a bedroom, tight, warm, and every inch drawn with stories, Rose finds her cousin Ann.

Pistol Ann was a good Punimin, with promise, and a heart of gold. The rope she hung herself with isn't what really killed her—

her heart died earlier today at the hand of the emissary. The noose she stretched around her neck might as well have been put there by him. The groove the rope scraped into the beam overhead is the last, if ugly, carving, and the last story, that this attic will ever hold. This room is finished now, finished by Ann. Finishing is the saddest thing Punimin ever know, and it's never meant to happen. You're always supposed to leave some space for tomorrow, but Ann couldn't do that for herself anymore. In disbelief, Rose watches her cousin, the woman she always wanted to be, hover from the rafters. Still. Broken. Dead. A grave statue built by the Strelkie. It's too late to do anything for Ann's lost life now, so Rose bows her head with a silent prayer, then hurries downstairs to tell her family.

Outside the Pistol home, this tiny shack in a giant, ancient forest where the fog hangs thickly, you can hear Madrick's screams for miles. The normally chatty night birds watch from their perches but say nothing. It's like they know. Madrick's echoing agony is not a fitting final song for his daughter, but in this land of King's Law, it's the one she is given.

CHAPTER
ROSE'S TIME IV

The next five years wind by slowly for the Pistol family, like a clock without numbers. Mourning seems to have no boundary. It's not enough time to forget. Though they try to live.

Pistol Rose is fifteen now. She gets into trouble one day and has her knuckles rapped for holding secret lessons training young boys how to fight in war. It doesn't matter that she's a Pistol—she's too young to instruct. It's her father's job to train the young men, and her uncle Madrick's job to train the young girls. (The training of girls was a position long held by Madrick's wife, Pistol Callory, until her untimely death in the forest. Whether she was murdered by a Strelkie soldier, eaten by a wilderucker, or ran away and disappeared for her own reasons is a mystery that no one can answer—but everyone knows not to talk about it. Madrick made up his own mind, and he buried an empty box. That was twelve years ago, and folks have felt mostly fine to let Madrick carry on performing his wife's duties, despite the occasional grousing from some Punimin women who covet the position. Training the girls how to act in war is more important than training the boys, depending on whom you ask. But for the most part, the Punimin have decided it's best to let Madrick be Madrick and not interfere.) Taking after her uncle, Rose continues giving boys additional training because she wants to—against the rules, in secret, in whatever hiding places she can find.

One by one, the boys stop coming, either because they keep getting caught and sentenced to gardening duty, or they grow tired of Rose's pointed affections at Clock Dancin. She's especially hard on him, and the other boys think it's love. Dancin *hopes* it's love, and he just wants to impress her, so he keeps sewing leather armor and making more accurate clocks as gifts for her—but no matter what he does, she keeps training him harder and harder, until her private classes are quit by everyone but him (none can keep up with Rose, and only Dancin tries) and they are left to wrestle and train together, alone. He can't do everything she teaches him, but instead of getting frustrated with his comparative lack of coordination, she's fascinated by his increasingly high-quality clock gadgets and leather armor. His gentle touch and mastery of a trade impresses her more than the stronger boys who sometimes try to make their way back into her secret classes. She quickly wallops those boys. And brave-necked girls who try to train with her are dispatched of almost as fast, because anyone who lays curious eyes on Dancin is in crucial need of a swift and unforgettable walloping. Rose never has to wallop a girl twice.

Over the years, their private battle armor, which can easily be hidden under clothes, becomes amended with drawn and carved stories of their childhood adventures together. Hunting rabbits, building a false wilderucker out of sticks, secretly irrigating Old Man Iron Gimmer's field after he lost his mind and forgot how to do it—then avoiding his switches and arrows for trespassing. All this time, their love is being forged and neither of them seems to understand what that means. They just know that if a clock's hands are turning, they turn best when they're around each other, especially with the grief of Ann still in the air like freshly cut grass, no matter the season. They keep their blades sharp, their wood cut, and their stories coming.

Their grief finally gives way one day when something wonderful, and dangerous, happens. Now, I counter the official histories and say the Fifth Age ends on *this* day—much sooner than the scribes report. They speak of widespread death and destruction and rebuilding. That's all true, but I stand by my mark because today is the true moment the Revolution is born. And the first time an idea sees light cannot be relegated to the footnotes. It is everything.

Pistol Rose is twenty now. She carries a basket of vegetables through her Punimin village. A little short-haired dog follows her. She plays with him, loses herself in joy with him, and ignores the increased Strelkie soldier presence all around as if it is a background growth of thorns she has learned to avoid, lest she wants to bleed.

Punimin carry on with their work and business, but the weight of the Strelkie eyes, ever present, saps them. Carvings on the outsides of buildings have been outlawed and replaced with bark—Strelkie find tree scales the best defense against graffiti and the easiest to replace. It gives the whole village a more uniform, though shaggy, look. The Punimin hate it, which makes the Strelkie love it, for they are short on creativity and long on cruelty. The only enduring happiness in this village seems to be a thin veil about Rose, and everyone wants to protect it like the last flower in the world—though Rose would be upset if she thought anyone was looking out for her or treating her like a favorite. She's got a severe streak of pride. She's a fighter and bashful of being doted upon, just like most Pistols, and shooting and fighting and hunting and war play are all that she keeps in front of her eyes.

Almost all. There is another thing. Suddenly, Clock Dancin, now twenty-two or so, leaps out—and hugs her. He kisses her neck. They've become an official couple, and loudly aware of their love. The years they spent being daft of their situation caused many Punimin mothers to worry if they were stupid. But lately, the ladies' eye rolling has lessened somewhat, and the gossipers (who are mostly men, and of that lot, more granddads than dads) have gotten giddy over these two.

"Are you looking for a fight, Mr. Clock Dancin?" Rose asks.

Dancin smiles. "I am, Miss Pistol Rose. Meet me in the grove. Hurry." He runs away.

She grins to herself. The Strelkie soldiers ignore them.

In a deep forest grove, Rose trots into a private, leafy pocket wearing leather armor and carrying a staff. This is a routine. "Face me, Mister! No dirty tricks, you cud."

Dancin pops out from behind a tree wearing a "fancy" suit with many family clocks on it. There's a blanket and picnic lunch nearby.

This isn't the training session she was expecting. She laughs. "Are you going to charm me to death?"

"Thought I'd try something new." He checks his pocket—oh

no. It's empty. She giggles as he rifles through more pockets. The pockets seem to be endless, and all of them empty.

"Lose something, Mister?"

He looks up—she's holding an engagement ring. She leaps to him and kneels, thrusts the ring into his hands. Their names are beautifully inscribed on it. His craftsmanship has improved tremendously since those first clumsy scribblings of her face on his fighting stick, especially his lettering.

"Rose—"

"Put your ring on my finger, boy."

"So you want to be my wife, Miss Pistol?"

"Yes, Mr. Clock, I do." She jumps onto him and kisses him like a hungry woodpecker until he laughs. Then she swats him— "You made that ring five months ago!"

He's aghast. "You knew?"

"Of course I knew! You think I'd spend all my waking hours with a man I didn't know inside and out?"

"Well. You don't know *everything*." He kisses her slowly and she falls out of time with him.

Behind a nearby thicket, a weaselly Strelkie soldier named Net Nesting pulls up his army trousers, careful not to make a sound. A half-naked, sultry Punimin girl called Teeth Molly dresses and follows him. (The Teeth clan boasts of a dozen generations of dentistry wisdom, but it isn't true: until fifty-six years ago they were simply known for biting, throwing fits, and generally acting like the forest's lesser-intelligent animals. None of this horrid behavior made it onto clocks, for obvious reasons, so their history isn't officially settled. But in truth, it wasn't until one of the boys managed to marry an educated girl named Candle Sally from Almyter that the Teeth began to resemble something respectable.

Molly, however, seems born to tug her family line backwards.) She has several polished bronze teeth that she claims are gold, unlike the rest of her family who all show off flawless pearly whites. Whereas Punimin generally find wood to carve, Molly has taken to her own skin with dyes and inks to tell stories—lies, really—of flying with crows. Her largest canvass is her shelfy bosom, which seems to have intentional difficulty fitting into every garment she selects. The ink she uses is allegedly "snake powder," a new substance of multiple uses being whispered about on the underground markets. Some people say it makes you crazy, if it's even real at all. Whatever Molly bought, snake powder or some imitation, it obviously made permanent marks on her skin, but if it made her crazier than she comes naturally, that would be hard to tell. They spy on Rose and Dancin.

Rose says, "Let's get married in secret."

"We could ask the district emissary," he offers gently. A sharp glare from her makes him rethink the suggestion. "I'm sorry—I know how your family feels about that, but if we go the secret way and the Strelkie find out, they'll come after everyone we love. That's war."

Net motions for Molly to hang back while he approaches like a cautious viper.

Rose says, "I'm not afraid of Strelkie. I'm just afraid of not living my life. I loved Ann, but I hate her for what she did. I won't do it. I won't bow to them. Do you know what sprawhammid is?"

Dancin squints searching for a school-time memory. "Is it what the ancients called brave adventurers?"

"I think so," she says. "But people nowadays say different things. Pig-headed fool, reckless pirate, stubborn noble. The more I hear about sprawhammid, the more it suits me. All together I think it really means to chase what you believe in, especially in the face of tyranny."

"And what do you believe in, Rose?"

"Love. It's what Punimin have and what Strelkie want to stamp out. It's freedom. It's choice. All those words we don't want to get overheard saying by the wrong people. If we say, 'sprawhammid' instead, we can be free to design our secrets openly, among our people. The Strelkie will never know. None are taught the word."

Dancin whispers, "Then our wedding will be sprawhammid."

Net Nesting blows a bone horn and startles them. He jumps out with a shiny shotgun. Teeth Molly leaps out with a rusty corkscrew knife. Psychos.

Net Nesting muses, "What do we have here?"

Teeth Molly shouts, "Lawbreakers! Them's treasonists!"

Net flexes his power. "Plotting to get married without consent of the district emissary?"

Molly looks stunned. "Wait. You're not the district em?" Did Molly just sleep with a *low* rank? She is perturbed.

Net shrugs her off. "No, but I work for him. I'll have his chair soon." He turns to Dancin. "I am Net Nesting. I reflect the district emissary. What you've spoken here is conspiracy of the sickest flavor."

Dancin attempts respect. "We were just planning to come and visit you—"

"Liars!" Molly shrieks. "We's heard your plots! What's heard can't be silent, not when it's rot. We'll make sure the authorities hear about this, what'd you call it, 'sprawhammid.' Your secrets is undone, they is."

Rose bites back. "Teeth Molly, I know your cousin; she's our dentist. Does she know you're carrying on with a Strelkie soldier?"

Molly's jaw drops. "Oh, ha ho! Blackmail? This cud just tried to blackmail me! Punish them! Stick them!"

Net looks unsure. Molly presses. "Punish them big, Net. I'll meet you up with my girlfriend if you do. She swings, love-dove. You just tell the story, and she'll play it for you." She points at a string of tattoos on her leg like a menu. They are ... enlightening to Net.

Net gulps and nods. "Okay. Okay, here's what we'll do. You come to my office later today and pay me to forget this."

Molly won't have that weakness. "You soft sludger, no! Punish them proper! Do it, Strelkie, or I'll tell the district em you're carrying on with a Punimin girl."

"He'd kill you too, stupid," Net snaps.

Molly rubs her neck sensually. "Not if he likes me. My bet's he will." Net turns shocked.

"Maybe we should all just go our separate ways," Dancin says.

Molly is on a roll now. "Nah, nah, nah. Make these cuds fight to the death. Barbellics style."

Net is in over his head with this girl.

Rose snarls, "Molly, what did I ever do to you?"

To Molly, everyone has wronged her. "Fight to the death. Tell them, Net! Tell!"

Net finds a courage he didn't know he had. "Whoever wins, their family lives. The loser's family dies with pain for conspiracy to host a wedding without permission. The emissary will want a strong example made."

Rose looks grave. "You can't be serious."

Molly jumps. "My man's serious, Pistol. And I gets the loser's head! I get to carry it on a post! The whole village will see I'm the top Punimin. Watch them buttoned-up doves look at me like a whore then. I'll see them gobble their words."

Net points his shotgun at Rose. "Fight now, or both families die. All of them."

Rose picks up her staff and looks to Dancin ....

Dancin nods. "You know what you have to do, Rose."

Rose ... pulls a cap off her staff—it's a spear. She throws her spear at Net and hits his gun—it falls and shoots lead near Molly's feet.

Molly squeals and runs away wailing for help—Net grabs his gun but Rose has her hands on it—Dancin joins their struggle. Net stabs Dancin in the leg and he falls away. Rose rolls with Net and climbs onto his back, uses his shotgun like a rod to choke him.

Net disassembles the gun like a puzzle trick and bucks her off his back. He runs and Dancin tackles him—Net reaches into his weapons belt pouch and strings a choke cable from it around Dancin's neck and strangles him. Rose jumps on and claws her fingers around Net's throat.

They didn't think it would be this hard. Together, Rose and choking Dancin drag Net toward a rock and bash his head against the ground with each step. It's a race to see which man falls unconscious first. Dancin turns blue—but Net blacks out!

Rose frees Dancin and says, "We have to get Teeth Molly, too."

Dancin nods, breathes, and staggers to his feet. Net groans. Rose clumsily reassembles his shotgun, not a Strelkie weapon she knows well, and shoots him dead.

Dancin is shocked. She tosses him the gun. "Come on!" Rose kicks her spear in an arc ahead of her, runs and catches it in stride. They hurry after Molly.

Molly loses her breath at the top of a canyon. She wasn't made for fighting, just the talk that starts it. Rose and Dancin catch up and corner her at the edge of a tall cliff. Big drop below.

Molly cries. "Why?!"

Rose approaches with steady feet, unyielding. "I'll make it fast."

Molly screams her guts out, "HELP! ANYBODY! PISTOL ROSE KILLED NET NESTING TO GET MARRIED! SHE'S GETTING MARRIED! SHE'S—"

It's peaceful and quiet at the bottom of the canyon. Until Molly lands dead on rocks. Rose's spear is stabbed through Molly's mouth, out the back of her head. Her face looks surprised.

Yes, it is dangerous to trifle with a cross Punimin. Some learn that the easy way. Some the hard.

Rose and Dancin return to the grove and drop Molly's body unceremoniously next to Net's. Dancin catches his breath and grumbles, "We should've left her at the bottom of the cliff. Covered her with rocks."

"No," Rose says. "That wouldn't guarantee she isn't found."

Dancin checks one of the many clocks on his person. Everyone in the Clock family has timepieces to spare, but never enough time. "I'll make a shovel out of bramblestick and bury them here. You should get back to the village before someone asks where you are."

Rose shakes her head. "We don't have caskets, so wilderuckers will dig them up. It's better to sink them in the river for the plick-erfish to eat."

"How do you know that?" He's a little scared to find out.

She tells him, "The Pistol family knows how to deal with Strelkie—my dad and my uncle do, anyway."

Dancin looks stunned. For a moment he thinks he doesn't recognize her, but then something tells him he always had a sense that she and her family had more war in them than they boasted.

She's nervous. "Now *you* know everything. Still want to get married?"

He kisses her. It's a promise. "Whatever we have to do. Sprawhammid."

"Sprawhammid," she says, like a whispered rally cry. Dancin admires the fight in her blood and wonders how much of that she will pass on to their children. A lot, he hopes.

Rose spots a necklace on Net's neck. Takes it. It's a bejeweled, simple, unimpressive thing of pearls and pewter, meant to look like a hand. She panics.

"What's wrong, Rose? What is that?"

"Net Nesting wasn't just another Strelkie soldier. This is a bloodline heirloom. He was an appointed cousin to Ward Harrol. We're knuckled."

The color drains from Dancin's face. "Wait—our assistant emissary is related to the king?"

"By decree. So, he made friends with someone important. Strelkie will come looking." Rose is frightened. Everything she wants may have just died with this rotten man. Killing him seemed like the only solution—the *right* solution—and now it may be their undoing.

Dancin struggles to find a path forward. "Then he got eaten by a wilderucker."

"We can't just leave him here! Soldiers will find him before a wilderucker does."

"Then we'll whittle and mar him up so it looks like a wilderucker killed him. Bring the body to the emissary."

Rose chuckles. "And win his favor? Maybe he'll even reward us with permission to marry?" Her eyes look wild.

"I was thinking that, yes. Rose, this doesn't look like an opportunity, but we can make it into one—"

She nearly turns to stone. "I'm not asking permission. Never ask me to do that again. We'll sink the bodies in the river and marry in secret. That's the wise course."

"I know it seems that way, but what if the Strelkie decide to torture our village until they get his body back?" Dancin is scared. His imagination is a wild horse when it gets spooked, and he never learned to control it.

But Rose is war-ready. "Let them try."

"Punimin don't want to go to war, and we can't make them! Not enough of them, anyhow. I would fight alongside you, and a few others would, I know. But no one did anything when the Strelkie killed two clans in Almyter for refusing to give up a baby. I've never even met a Punimin from the wood dunes or peninsulas, and I know the Punimin from the ranges never leave their plains. I don't know what it would take to make the Punimin rise up. We'd need a revolution." Dancin kicks a stone. Rose thinks.

Perhaps the word "revolution" sticks to her now; perhaps this is the precise moment it begins. Perhaps this is where "sprawhammid" becomes more than naughty rebellious slang to her, more than a fun inside-word between two people in love. Perhaps this is where "revolution" and "sprawhammid" are wed, even if she doesn't know it yet.

Dancin offers, "We can sink Molly and tell a tale—no one dangerous will ask after us—but they need Net Nesting's body. If his corpse comes from us, we win favor for finding it. Our emissary grants marriage eight times out of ten anyway."

"He does not," Rose insists. "That's a Strelkie statistic. Always divide a Strelkie statistic by a hundred because they exaggerate."

"Rose, he *is* lenient. *Permission is freedom.*"

She shakes her head. "Dancin, no, it is not. If the emissary declines us, we'd have to run away and take our families with us. That's a lot of people, and I don't know if you've noticed, but my family tends to be war-headed."

"Yeah ... leaving *would* be hard."

"Like eating a mountain," she says.

"But it won't come to that, Rose. We'll get permission and live freely in our own country. Net's body is a coin. Let's spend it. This way we don't put everybody at risk. The Strelkie have taken enough."

Rose considers Net's body, and Molly's. "Anything we do is a risk. If we twist up a lie and get caught, we'll be branded 'carvers.'" That is the worst insult she can imagine. Though every Punimin does carve *wood* or *stone* often, one does not use that word—and if they do use it, they do so carefully. Handmade storytelling has no name. Calling attention to it by voice ruins it, and so "carving" is the ugliest term a Punimin can endure, especially when it is assigned to their character. Killers are cleaner folk. Carvers are liars. Every family has a different sense of what honor means, but regardless of what that is, few worries outweigh it.

Dancin simmers. "I would never let that disrespect tie to your family."

"If you had power like that, we wouldn't have worries. But you don't, and we do. How to fix this problem isn't up to you. Or me. It's a family decision now."

After they quickly sink Molly's body in a river under stones, they return and Rose folds Net's body in half at the hips and lashes him to a long stick. They cut down some corn stalks from a field and weave them over the corpse to make it look like a fat bundle of crops tied to the stick. Each carries one end and they walk home in the open like plain farmers. None pay them mind; all have their own troubles these days. All have their own fears about the future.

In the Pistol family cottage, David, Grace, Beau, Rose's now-grown sister Jennifer, and Madrick look at Net's dead body on the floor, before Rose and Dancin. Jennifer polishes a bone-and-steel revolver of her own making.

Dancin finishes catching everyone up. "This way we don't put everybody at risk."

Rose's father David asks, "Rose, does the Clock family know you intend to wed?"

Dancin interrupts Rose. "My family doesn't know anything yet, sir. They're not fighters like you. They're tradespeople."

Uncle Madrick turns grumpy. He has taken to drink and anger. "*We're* tradespeople. We craft hunting weapons so powerful and intimidating they could make the Valorickans of the

North sweat in the cold. We make answers for dangers, kid. You make ... fancy watches. The sun works just as well for telling time."

"Yes," Dancin says, "but we can also tell time in the rain ... sir."

Madrick glares at him, but with a slight twinkle.

Rose offers the old saying, "'The more wild, the more fruitful.' By all judgements that matter, we're a proper match." She puts a gentle hand on Madrick's arm. "And you don't have to worry about the Clocks. Every Punimin's a fighter when need be. We just thought keeping this to must-know-only was the rightful path now."

David looks to his wife Grace for input. She's a bundle of nerves struggling to stay held together. She says, "I don't see what the Clock family contributes to Punimin, frankly. The family clocks make wonderful stories, but so do our walls and ceilings. Crafting peacetime tickers and gadgets doesn't protect anyone from the troubles. Strelkie have no end of gizmos and it doesn't keep anguish from them either. It might cause it—and you know that spreads."

Dancin knows this is his moment to prove himself. "I love your daughter, Ma'am. I would kill and die for her." The Pistols consider Net's body on the floor.

Grace judges Dancin. It's a thorough stare and everyone lets her take her time ... "Okay, that's one Clock I can like."

"That wasn't bad, kid," Madrick says. "First thing you said worth hearing. Keep doing that."

Dancin offers, "We'll be careful who we tell and how we talk about it. We're calling it 'sprawhammid.'"

Madrick smiles at that, but Grace looks ill. "Against the tide," she mutters to herself with disdain.

David asks Grace, "Are you willing to sail to Afar if this goes side-bottom?"

She looks bothered like only a wife with a stubborn husband can look. She answers in her best (and failing) effort to sound unbothered, "Have your jungle friends written you back?"

Pistol David's face betrays the answer: no.

Grace decides, "Forget the Jungle Country, then. We can hide deeper in the forest. We have the make-how to live wild if need be."

"Like the Pipers and Remfords?" David isn't a fan of the Pipers and Remfords. Swamp folks.

Rose's cousin Beau is on David's side. "I heard they were eaten alive by wilderuckers."

Grace retorts, "Yes, well, apparently that's the risk you take. Better to be dead than told what to do, right, David?" She gives David a cutting look since her stab at being unbothered and subtle didn't win. She doesn't like his big ideas—but can't say that, because he could point to numerous occasions on which she fell in love with his big ideas. They settle on him smiling and her scowling.

Rose's sister Jennifer asks, "But if you get permission, we'll stay?"

"That's right, Jennifer," Dancin says. "We don't want to cause trouble unless we have to."

Madrick sneaks a glance at Rose. He knows trouble-picking is in her blood, and he's bemused by watching her bite her tongue to go along with Dancin's attempt at peace here. Madrick doesn't imagine this cool-headed side of Rose will stick for long, and that amuses him even more. Somehow he manages not to laugh.

Pistol Jennifer looks contemplative, keeps polishing her gun.

"We already know what it will be like to stay here, though, and that every day ahead doesn't look as bright as those behind—for the whole continent. But the jungle island sounds nice."

Beau is suddenly frightened. "It's across the Beast Sea. Water doesn't come by that name without good reasons."

Jennifer twirls her gun, holsters it, then finds another one to clean. She assures Beau, "It's worth crossing. Afar doesn't have King's Law. They might even let you run around naked. You could get over your shyness *and* meet men who actually find you attractive."

Beau quickly calculates how the rest of his life might play out. "All excellent points. Well ... anything's better than being a Strelkie. And that's pretty much what we are now. I'm for whatever Cousin Rose wants. Dad, what say you?"

All eyes turn to Madrick. He's whittling a knuckle shield into the face of his late daughter, Ann. Were his fist to land on a cheek, the subject's visage would then bear a stamp of Ann. Madrick announces, "You know my feelings. Even if the son of a bitch grants permission, I think we should kill him. *That's* what sprawhammid means, and I'm all for it."

Grace wavers. "All of our friends live here. I don't like the idea of anyone getting hurt, or hiding all their life. No war. I'd rather things just work out as we want." She stands, sees she's the only squeaky wheel here. "But if things can't go as we'd choose, maybe your father will hear back from his jungle pen pals. He's had some long luck before, I admit it."

David smiles at her. She scowls, but only to hang onto her pride. She continues, "You children won't remember, but my grandmother, Tanner Hildegard, always said, 'You live longer if you just take things more as they are.' She kept her head down, did what anyone with authority told her to do, and she lived a long, long life ... died of boredom." Grace slaps her hand on the table loudly and shakes her head as if to shrug off the bad smell of a dark daydream—she doesn't intend to become her grandmother. As many times as she catches herself acting like that old sour sheep, and as hard as her roots fight to stick her to that dusty ground, her willpower is stronger than blood or history. She is brave. Or so she wishes. "If my children want to live in a jungle, or on a boat, or at hell's gate, I'm the mom and it's my job to secure property there. We'll go wherever we have to, if that's what we need to do."

Rose beams. "Thank you, Mom."

Grace touches Rose's hand on her way to hug Dancin. She holds him tightly, almost a threat. She grabs a handful of clocks on him like a leash. "Welcome to the family. You just be sure the emissary says yes. That's what's best for Rose and all of us. I don't want *anybody's* idea of sprawhammid playing out, no matter how mild you think it is. You don't want to see me go to war. Understood?"

Dancin nods. Grace knows he's scared and can't promise her anything, but she appreciates that he means to. That's enough for her, that his heart is built the right way. She touches his cheek. "Very good then, son. Very good. Because the last place I want any of us to be is in the crosshairs of our vile and slack-witted king."

SIMPLE PIG-BARBARISM

CHAPTER V

I remember a great orator telling the story I tell you now. There is a castle-like dungeon. High thin windows, unreachable, but barred nonetheless. A domed ceiling lined with ornate stained-glass depictions: the history of our previous Age, the Fourth Age: pirate battles on high seas, serpents and monsters, battlefields, magicians using potions and experimenting on beasts—all of this exaggerated and glorified as if to teach children lessons. Ornamentation is the only survivor of that Fourth Age, and I often thought how much prettier it is to look at now than it must have been to live it then.

There is a jury box of eight perfectly randomized Strelkie citizens, dressed in high fashion and bright colors, sitting straight as though at school. They, and a foul, robed judge with a mangy beard atop his towering desk-podium of blood-red marble, watch the great and talented lawyer Toir Pat, a man dressed in a standout theater suit with a ceremonial breastplate boasting doves, and pirate scarves tied at his neck and arms to symbolize his academic accomplish-

ments—like intellectual scalps. He considers his next words with musical care ...

He says, "Dames and Gents of the jury, my fellow Strelkie, Your Honor—I apologize if my language, 'slack-witted,' regarding the king has offended. I only mean to illustrate the corrupt and deviant point of view of the accused Punimin here, the one we caught."

Dirty hands stick out of an iron box, shackled. The identity of this prisoner is obscured in heavy shadows. Toir Pat continues, "It is my job to defend this scrapper-claw, no matter how revulsive we find it."

The angry judge nods and calms down a little. Toir Pat is a passionate fellow. "It is my job to make you—briefly, wrongly *even—see the world as this criminal defiler does. So that you may decide guilty, or innocent, with the fullest understanding of how deep the corruption goes, how twisted is the thinking that caused this crime—this most profound of nearly unspeakable crimes, this sprawham-mid, against our beloved god-king and our cherished,* correct *way of life."*

The judge yells, "Hear, hear!"

Toir Pat thinks himself eloquent. "For the Punimin are different from you and me. Only one of us is pure in spirit—it's true."

The jurists all nod. Toir Pat delivers with an impassioned might, "Why did our god-king promise the best of us immortality, but the Punimin get nothing? Why is the city mighty but the forest abandoned to chaos and savagery? Because the Punimin don't believe in trusting those righteously placed in power. They trust only their experience of the world. *They believe* they *have the answers. They believe* they *should have power. They believe* they *should make their* own *clocks and keep their* own *time. As if our wise god-king,*

the brightest light in all the known Four Continents, wasn't enough.
As if King's Law wasn't enough. Imagine."

The judge chuckles. Toir Pat nods. *"I agree with the prosecutor:*
my criminal client did what was done to spit in the face of King's
Law. To knuckle the king himself. All Punimin are like ungrateful
children after frog candy, only worse. *They are simpler than our*
barbaric enemies to the east, more foolish than our arrogant neigh-
bors to the north, and more cavemen than the cuds to the south. The
Punimin are rabid for their reckless so-called independence and
their brainless, simple pig-barbarism."

The prosecutor snickers. Toir Pat smiles. *"There is nothing more*
apt to draw a Punimin into a crime of conspiracy to topple our king-
dom, which this was, *than telling them 'what to do.' There is*
nothing worse to them than being asked to request that their loving
district emissary allow a marriage. Marriage, *which* we *Strelkie*
know is a failed model of societal unity—just look at the failed states
and savages filling the other continents—but that we graciously
allow the Punimin to keep as a pacifier out of our abundant generos-
ity. No—the Punimin hate us for that."

I remember Toir Pat as a clever man. A carver, but a damned
good one.

THE SHARPER
THE PLANS

CHAPTER
VI

Today a *new* district emissary, the impossibly skinny Silo Countant, who seems to have too many elbows, wears medallions like a breast full of ornaments, each one praising him for some alleged kindness, reviews a stack of jewelry with boney fingers and abundant disdain as he simultaneously flits through paperwork in this old, crummy office. He's much like the previous emissary, only with a meaner temperament and something to prove. Dancin and the Pistol family stand awaiting his decision over their requested permission. Only Pistol Madrick is absent from these proceedings, which all agree is for the best—he scarcely bites his tongue when he has *little* to say. These days, the man could spit a tome.

Emissary Countant smirks, "Your payment is a bit scant. But we have much gratitude for this." He gestures to Net's mutilated body on the floor with a knotty elbow. "I'd like to see a wilderucker. Is it true they're just illegal Punimin offspring who spent too much time in the trees? Or were they created by you people mating with foul creatures? Like how termites came into being. It's a sincere question."

Beau offers, "Whatever they are, they're very hard to catch. I've only seen one in my whole life."

Countant sighs. "It's a shame I wasn't there to witness this alleged mauling."

Everyone holds their breath, nervous. Countant muses, "Net Nesting was a moth stain who deserved worse. I bet he squealed. Oh, that would have been a song to remember." Countant snickers a snotty little chortle. It reminds Rose of a time she thought she saw a piglet laughing. She finds it so odd that such a skinny man can be so piglike. But his feelings toward Net Nesting, bizarre as they may be, align with their purpose and bring relief to all their faces.

David offers, "You should burn the body. You don't want to touch wilderucker bites—"

"Enough of that, thank you." Countant gets lost in his own thoughts, which are always the most interesting things to him. "I'm just thinking ... your payment here. Hmm."

Grace politely says, "It's everything we have. May I ask where the usual emissary is today?"

Countant chuckles that tiny swine laugh again. "Contributing to your soil with everything he has. He was executed for being too lenient. I'm Silo Countant, the new top decider for this territory. You're extremely lucky to have me. I actually follow the law."

Rose and Dancin trade a nervous look. David touches a gun tucked behind his back. Grace grabs him firmly to halt.

Countant makes his decision. "Alright. I'll grant your request for marriage and the record will *show that*, so you can all stop claiming that King's Law is 'evil.'"

They all look like a weight was just lifted. But he continues. "However. Ward Harrol promised to provide a somewhat disliked foreign ally with soldiers for a new war. It's quite interesting, actually—an independent island west of the Southern Fire Straits is having trouble with the Pirate Sisters. The king has agreed to march twelve-thousand men along the enemy Fire Straits' coastline to then build a Strelkie fort to support ships near this island. It will be a historic campaign if it succeeds; we've never been able to build a fort in Fire Straits territory because the savages are so ... creatively persistent. The king is populating the bulk of the order with Punimin men instead of Strelkie soldiers—who'd rather not leave home right now. So, your marriage is off-the-record revoked, as Clock Dancin must bequeath himself to war."

Dancin protests, "But—sir, I'm not a soldier. I'm a clockmaker."

"Oh, I think the brush will survive with a slightly smaller output of clocks for the foreseeable future. And don't worry about your service responsibilities, boy, you just have to catch your share of bullets and flame to protect the construction officers. It isn't hard." Countant couldn't care less. "Report for duty in two weeks. Failure to do so will result in the removal of hands for all the men in your family, and capital punishment for two of your women via 'tearing.' If any of you help this cud avoid King's Law, the Clock family and the Pistol family will be executed in Strelkie City's public square in, shall we say, an entertaining fashion." Countant stands. "Congratulations. You have a place in the king's army. Your contribution will be recorded as a number in the next *Book of Ward Harrol's Reign*. That's a hitherto unknown honor for Punimin."

Outside in the Punimin village, the Strelkie soldier occupation has grown thicker. But the Pistol family's walk of defeat and fear hasn't changed much since ten years ago. Rose feels herself slipping toward thoughts of Ann dangling in the attic. Then she swears to herself that she'll never set foot in that attic again.

David whispers, "Clock Dancin."

Dancin walks next to Pistol David. Rose stays close by. David mutters under his breath, "Your family builds watches and calendars. Anything else?"

Dancin nods. "My grandma comes from a hunting family that makes weapons. We *can* fight, sir. It's just keeping time is what we're best at."

David considers. "Well ... keeping time is important when you have precise work to do and only two weeks to do it."

Rose asks, "You mean like planning a wedding?"

David looks at the watching Strelkie soldiers to make sure they're far enough away that they can't hear. "I mean exactly like planning a wedding. And an escape."

Rose hugs her father. He says to Dancin, "Set a meeting with your family. We'll need to make an impression."

"Yes, sir," Dancin says.

Rose is nervous. "Dad? What kind of impression?"

David smiles wickedly.

The Punimin have an old church on the opposite end of their village from where the Strelkie soldiers camp and watch them. The outside has been tacked with shaggy bark by Strelkie to make it look as plain as possible and quite uncarvable. But inside, it is a tiny wooden cathedral where every surface has carvings and reliefs of village history through the ages as witnessed by an elderman: weddings, births, funerals, parties, rare visits from Punimin of the ranges and wood dunes. Tonight there isn't a religious service, nor is there an elderman present (Elderman Jones Hallow is out visiting cousins in Almyter; he loaned the church keys to Pistol David so he could oil the benches and keep the whittlers honest). But none of that is going on tonight—tonight this building is only in the service of conspiracy and rebellion.

The Clock family waits in pews. They are granddad Wyatt, grandma Francine, mother Leslie, father Rollo, Dancin's younger sister Zoe, and Dancin's older brother Ejjer. They're all dressed in fancy formalwear to make a good impression, with their finest watches on display—but not *so* on display as to look like they're their *best* clocks, even though they of course are.

The Clocks make up a peaceful, mindful lot. Ejjer is the bad egg of the family, but by choice. He's a sorrowful young man in need of happiness, and in need of fewer secrets than he keeps. He's outrageously attractive but emotionally tortured. His parents don't know what to do with him. But that's not why they're here tonight.

Papa Rollo checks one of the fancier watches clung to his vest. It tells the story of a rabbit outrunning a lion once every hour. "The Pistols are late. Interesting."

Dancin's little sister Zoe says, "Papa, be nice."

Papa Rollo grumbles, "Making tea is a useful, punctual profession. My most promising son couldn't marry a girl from the notably punctual Tea Tribe?" He taps on a floorboard carved with images of tea makers. "The Clocks will unite with the Pistols?" He points at a pillar showing a Pistol of olden days firing a gun and wailing like a wild beast. "Detestable."

Grandma Francine smacks Rollo's head. He chuckles. She says sternly, "There's nothing wrong with the Pistol family, Rollo. Enough."

Rollo shakes his head. "They're a fighting family. Fighting's not a trade. Making clocks, making tea—those are valuable contributions to Punimin."

Granddad Wyatt doesn't pause his whittling on the armrest of a pew, but suggests, "Listen to your mother, son."

Grandma Francine yowls, "Now that would be a valuable contribution!"

Rollo mutters, "Bullnagie." His wife Leslie tickles him for swearing. He giggles.

Dancin's brother Ejjer complains, "How long is this meeting, and what kind of gift are they bringing?"

His mother Leslie says, "They said it was a welcome gift, Ejjer. Make sure you compliment whatever it is."

Bored Ejjer sarcastically salutes his mother with a single finger. She points at him like a threat to behave. Judging from his smile, her threat doesn't take.

The doors bang open: the Pistols are all bloody, muddy, carrying weapons—and a body: *dead Clock Dancin.*

It's a terrible shock. The Pistols set Dancin's body down on the floor and the Clocks surround him. He's a gorged mess, barely recognizable. They're in complete hysterics. How could this be happening?

Pistol David says, "Wilderucker. Came out of nowhere."

Dancin watches from the shadows. He's not dead. That's not his body—though the hair and the part of the face that remains do bear an uncanny resemblance. Rose looks at her father to end this charade. This is no joke worth seeing through.

But David continues, "All he wanted was to marry Rose."

"I'll marry her." It's Ejjer. He's quite earnest and raw. It's almost embarrassing to see him bare his soul. "I'll marry you. For Dancin. For our families. I'm the only Clock who can, now. Dancin wasn't a real Clock anyway; he was adopted."

Clock Leslie scowls at Ejjer, who couldn't be more serious. "Look, our story can go right here," Ejjer points at a bare spot on a pillar carved with brides and grooms. "I've known you all my life, Rose. Well, I've known *about* you, at least."

Pistol Madrick busts up laughing and can't stop. The Clocks look aghast. Beau laughs. David gives it up: "I think we made our impression."

Dancin sheepishly steps out of hiding—his mother Leslie shrieks. Ejjer runs up and punches him in the arm, hard. "What was that, Dancin!"

Papa Rollo is furious. "Yes. What was that?"

Pistol David explains, "We need to make the emissary think Dancin's dead. How'd we do?"

Grandma Francine bursts out, "Very convincing."

Madrick grins at her. "Welcome to the Pistol family! We're swell-good at convincing. You can trust that."

Ejjer looks to his mother. "Should I compliment the welcome gift now, or wait until it starts to stink?" Leslie swats him.

Granddad Wyatt is bemused and puts his carving knife away. "Who was that man? Who did you kill?"

Pistol Jennifer answers, "A Strelkie soldier who had a reputation for eyeing little girls, and more than eyeing."

Ejjer doesn't like any of this. "Why do the authorities need to think Dancin is dead?"

Dancin claps Ejjer on the back. "It went side-bottom. They ordered me to war in two weeks, brother. It's not a war to stop anything; it's a war to start more trouble. And it's a death sentence. They said as much."

Their mother Leslie is aghast. "No. They can't just do that to you. They have their *own* people."

The Clocks are horrified, except Ejjer—he likes the idea. "You're going to be a Strelkie soldier?"

"He's not," Rose assures. "We want to get married and leave for Afar."

That hits the Clocks with weight. Clock Zoe is the youngest and most curious. "The Jungle Country? Is it real?"

Pistol David proudly holds a letter the size a bird carries. "I have trusted old friends from childhood who went there. Feather Joy and Feather Patrick. They've wed with some nativeborn, and my communication has extended to some of their dominant tribe and trusted friends. They have just secretly extended the warmest invitation for both our families." Grace rubs his back affectionately. He couldn't be prouder.

Rose has it all worked out. "If Dancin is killed by a wilderucker and I drown or hang myself, the Strelkie won't look for us. We've already picked out a lady soldier who could pass for me. They call her 'The Impaler.' She's the one who killed Firelock Gillen and tore up those children over in Bearfield."

Granddad Wyatt frowns, a thoughtful and calculating man. "How do you know for sure that faking your own deaths will play?" His eyes aren't too old to spot the story of a younger Rose drowning a Strelkie soldier on the hilt of her knife.

Rose sets her hand there. "We know it, sir."

Granddad Wyatt respects something he senses in her face, then whispers some serious business with his wife Francine.

Ejjer tries to redirect everyone. "Dancin serving in the king's army would be good for our family. That would give us status. Where is the war, in the Southern Fire Straits?"

Dancin is easily annoyed by his brother. "I'm not serving a false god-king, Ejjer."

Ejjer gets mad. "You were born Strelkie anyway. The nurses on the Line gave you to Mom by mistake. I'll *never* have this opportunity—"

Dancin almost spits. "Ejjer, the king's orders can burn."

Papa Rollo pleads, "Dancin, the Clock family doesn't cause trouble with the law. We're not bandits or rabble-rousers."

Madrick takes pride in those terms. "No. That you're not." He chuckles when he realizes his butt is half-sitting on a carving of a clock. Not the most respectable arrangement, but fitting, to him.

Dancin argues, "What if the law causes trouble, Papa? We can't accept that. But we can all go to Afar."

Clock Leslie shakes her head. Not going to happen. Rollo pulls Dancin aside but speaks loudly enough that the Pistols are sure to hear, "These Pistols are monsters. This was a sick joke."

Grace tries to calm Rollo down. "My husband and his brother don't understand what 'having fun' means."

Rollo flusters like he's an angry hen and doesn't accept Grace's run at an apology. Granddad Wyatt bangs his cane on the floor and stands. The carvings on his cane are *perfect*—piles of nude bodies clamoring over each other for the top of the cane. A bizarre, frightening, but poignant image. It always makes him think twice about how hard he's willing to chase after something and really consider what it is. "My wife is going to speak now." That steals the room. Wyatt sits.

All turn to Clock Francine. She's the boss. Her gown shimmers with a design handstitched out of melted pieces of Strelkie inventions turned into beads and discs. No Punimin warrior wears as much stolen Strelkie material as Francine; no Punimin has earned the right to as much as she has. "Ward Harrol claims to be a one-hundred-and-fifty-seven-year-old god-king. And the Strelkie believe it! I've known a Strelkie or a few."

Granddad Wyatt looks at the floor. He doesn't like her pain. She continues. "I know what they promise, and what they actually give."

Granddad Wyatt takes her hand. A dark past there, but private. She warns, "The trouble you propose causing could lead to a proper fight."

Pistol Madrick nods heavily and somberly.

Grandma Francine continues, "There's an ancient word for people with fire guts and eager minds to rally to war with a cause they feel is just."

"Sprawhammid," Pistol Grace mutters.

Grandma Francine nods at her, surprised she knows the term. Francine says, "I cannot condone going to war with the Strelkie, though they deserve it. The great old Pistols, the Irons, and the Teeth tried to start up something when I was a young girl." This is news to most of them: as a boy, David had heard whispered snatches of rebellious Pistols past, but such stories were always hushed, dismissed as little more than flights of pride and fancy, exaggerations engraved on clocks ... but what if they were true?

"They tried to start something *big*," Francine continues, "but the Strelkie never lose a fight. The Punimin of the wood dunes and the ranges and the peninsulas knew that only too well and did not come to aid. They saw the blood spilled but stuck to their own concerns at home. A lot of Pistols, Irons, and Teeth died thinking they were sprawhammid, thinking they were righteous warriors. Or noble poets. Or whatever in between. It's fun to rally and fight and rebel, at first ... but our people, even just our people here in the wilderness, have never been organized enough to see a war through to any end besides regret. No one's ever even agreed *what* 'sprawhammid' means. It originally meant to be on a quest to find God. Somehow that became a quest to find war, and love, and even self-aggrandizement. I see all of those things in us now. I'd like to think it would be different this time, but Strelkie are unified under one leader. We're not and never have been. Each Punimin region, each Punimin family, has a different interest. Each home keeps its own time. Our people are like a clock with a *thousand*-thousand disagreeing hands. But the Strelkie obey one mind with one hand—one hand honed into a fist—and they all practice an obsession on warring. We'd swiftly lose again. They would burn us to ash. Only the scribes would win, because 'sprawhammid' would finally have one definition, and it would be something about our tragic defeat."

David and Madrick look stern and ready to argue—though Francine has more to say. "But ... all that being said, I can't help wonder if the jungle wouldn't enjoy, or dare I say benefit from, the skills this generation of Pistols and Clocks possess. Probably they could at least use a talented talker like me."

Clock Leslie argues, "Mother, we can't just move to Afar—"

"It's quite simple. We've been invited, so we can leave here and go there. And we shall." Grandma Francine is the last word, and there's nothing Leslie can do to change that. Francine says, "A secret and illegal wedding—hidden deep in the forest of course—an event that flaunts every stupid and humiliating law they shove down our throats—now, that's a party a gal can get excited about. That's a just, proper, and right sprawhammid to me." She hugs Rose. "Welcome to the Clock family, dear." And that seals it.

Pistol David offers his hand to Clock Leslie and tells her, "I've been told my having fun isn't amusing to everyone. I don't understand what's not funny about tricking folks that someone's dead —but if it was my tone, or you found my presentation coarse or something, I apologize."

Leslie looks to Pistol Grace, who offers a reconciliatory nod. Leslie accepts David's hand of apology. "It was a fine gift that made a fine point that we needed, and I won't forget it, Pistol. You've given us a fresh opportunity at a free future that I'm sure we'll make the most of. If it isn't scary, it's probably not worth doing. I haven't been scared in some time. So, thank you."

Madrick gives Rollo a flask. "Brought you some tea, Clock."

Rollo sniffs the flask. "Tea, you say?"

Madrick smiles. "Aye. 'Tea.'"

Rollo sips. He reacts like it is stinging fire water. He loves it.

Madrick confesses, "With maybe a hint of rum."

"A hint? Or half a holler?"

Madrick chuckles. "A holler—a full holler. Or two."

"That's against King's Law." Rollo laughs. Madrick laughs back. And like that, these men are friends. Rollo toasts. "To Clock Dancin and Pistol Rose! To the first wedding in five years!"

David leaps up. "And the biggest wedding Punimin ever shoved up the Strelkie's ass!" His vulgarity stuns everyone. Then

Grandma Francine claps thunderously and Granddad Wyatt whoops. It's in that moment that they realize their village holy man, Elderman Jones Hallow, has returned from his vacation. He is old, bearded, dressed simply with a single long rifle on his back and a sash on his belt indicating his trade of prayer. And, unusually, he also carries a small birdcage on his back, shrouded with a black cloth. He was given a strange pet by his cousins in Almyter, and ordinarily that would be the talk of the evening. But this is clearly a special night, so he tucks his birdcage into a dark and quiet closet to let his little traveling companion sleep. He looks like a bemused parent discovering his children throwing a secret party.

"What did I miss?" he asks.

That night, the Clocks and the Pistols dance, drink, and party. Elderman Hallow enjoys being caught up on all the conspiracy. He loves gossip, but planning and plotting make him feel alive. Leslie and her daughter Zoe play music for them with a violin and pipes. Their feet stomp like drums.

But Ejjer hangs off to the side, concerned about this wedding. But not about the dead body—the fake-death-Dancin body, that he dragged into the woods and hid moments ago after volunteering to do so. He made a proper job of it and was happy to do it, but there's a storm in his mind and a pit in his stomach over their foolish misunderstanding of "sprawhammid."

Meanwhile, grandma Francine finishes telling Rose a story worthy of laughter. She dotes on Rose. Dancin politely steals Rose away for a private talk and says, "They're going to invite the whole village."

"That's a terrible idea. We'll get caught," Rose whispers.

"The Punimin who work as servants in the city, some of them have made friends with Strelkie. They could start whispers and rumors among the Strelkie that Punimin occasionally go on night-long hunting holidays that pull entire villages miles away from home."

"Holidays?" Rose asks. "Strelkie don't even know what holidays are. They don't have them."

Dancin shrugs. "But they know we do."

"I don't know if the Strelkie will believe it."

"It doesn't matter as long as they can't find us," he says. "It's happening. This isn't about us anymore. Our moms can't stop our dads from inviting people. And now that our elderman is involved, it's a holy mission to spread the winds of freedom—or something. I'm not sure exactly how he meant to put it; he's quite drunk."

Elderman Hallow laughs large as Granddad Wyatt tells an old story that makes Grandma Francine blush and swat him. "I'm stealing that story!" Elderman Hallow yells.

Rose sighs. "At least it's only our village."

"Well," Dancin mutters, "they also invited some clans from Bearfield. And from way over in Almyter. Also, Elderman Hallow wants to invite holy men from the peninsulas and ranges and wood dunes, too."

"Oh, so just the entire continent?" Rose mutters.

"Not the entire continent. Just people *from* the entire continent," Dancin says.

"This is fantastic," she says sarcastically. "Is it too late to simply get married tonight with just the people here?"

Dancin whispers, "That was never possible. Our mothers would skin us, and Elderman Hallow would refuse on principle. Punimin party as surely as birds sing and snakes bite. That cannot be changed."

"You're right," she says. "This isn't about us anymore."

"But if the Strelkie find out, they'll kill everyone we know."

Wyatt pulls Francine into a dance. Rose knows Dancin is right; the Strelkie would kill everyone. She tells him, "So, we just have to get away with it."

"We know how to fake our deaths," he says.

"That's the easy part. We can disappear and our families can leave, but all of Puniminkind can't vanish to Afar. If so much as a word of this leaks, what will they do?"

Rollo and Madrick yell loudly and dance together, drunk and rambunctious.

Dancin doesn't know if they can get away with their plan. Not when their families act like this. They could draw attention from the furthest hills. "We should go deep into the forest."

"Very deep," Rose says. "A hidden place not on any Strelkie map. Where voices and song don't carry."

"Quite a trick," Dancin says. "Our plans have to be sharp."

"Sharper than clockwork," she agrees. "Nothing can tick sideways. No one can make a mistake."

Ejjer is suddenly upon them. "Dancin, may I dance with Rose?"

Dancin doesn't like this idea. Rose puts a friendship bracelet on Ejjer's wrist. Beaded and nutted, just like the one she gave to Lilly years ago.

"Ejjer," she says kindly, "this is a token of friend-being. I'll make them for all my in-laws if it's not silly. Will you see what everyone thinks before I risk it? Get honest opinions."

Dancin and Rose dance away. Ejjer watches, bereft. He doesn't know if he's embarrassed, ashamed, or jealous. He just knows he's mad.

Pounding on the front door. The music stops and the Pistols and Clocks rush out the backdoor—except Ejjer, who hides. Elderman Hallow snatches his cloaked birdcage and is quick out of the room just before the front door bursts open. Strelkie soldiers hurry in with torches and hunt around. One of them announces, "There was alcohol here. It smells like a holler's worth, at least."

Their leader says, "But the bigger crime is using a closed church. They know we shuttered this building. Burn it, then find someone at random to punish."

Ejjer crawls under pews as smoke begins to billow. He manages to worm into a vent. He crawls and slithers his way outside. He runs away as the church beflames. Punimin hurry to gather and watch it burn, all horrified, none willing to be the first to fight one of the Strelkie soldiers feeding the fire with any possessions Punimin happened to leave outside. Elderman Hallow is tempted to use his rifle on them, but he would only get one or two before they cut him down and made life that much worse for the Punimin here. Instead of fighting now, he'll use the moment for a speech at his next service. No matter his pain, no matter the darkness he faces, standing up in front of people afterwards makes him feel better. He feeds on these moments, to a fault. Maybe one day he'll raise his fist. He counts on it.

Something squeaks and startles him. He remembers he's

holding the birdcage at his side, and lifts the black shroud to check on his little friend from Almyter. It's not a bird he's been given, not exactly. It's an endangered flycub, a miniature lioness baby, golden-brown and smaller than a five-pound kitten, with a set of wings. This little girl stretches her front legs, arches up her butt and tail, and unfolds and flutters her feathered wings, each of which is proportioned larger than her body and struggles to wave in the cage when extended. She squawks at him fiercely to feed her, then rubs her face against the cage and purrs. She's sassy and adorable; her ears are too large for her head, and though she wants to be a lioness, right now she's so little that a large mouse could bully her. If she were released from the cage, she would fly gracelessly and crooked, like a new bat, calling with a raspy meow that she would think is a roar. All she wants to do is fly, eat, and take naps on laps. Elderman Hallow's Almyter cousins gave him this little runt to shepherd. Flycubs are rumored to have been created by scientists in the Fourth Age, but were hunted to near extinction by both men and wileruckers, and now male flycubs are incredibly hard to find. Elderman Hallow doesn't just have to feed this little girl; he's also promised to look in this part of the continent for a male flycub to mate with her. He doesn't think it will happen; he'll just be happy if he can keep her from getting eaten by a wilerucker or "collected" by some Strelkie who mis-imagines what she might look like as a full-grown adult (people assume flycubs grow large, but they almost always top out at ten or twelve pounds).

Despite his intent to care for her, their relationship has been fraught with annoyance on both sides. "Not now, Teacup," he tells her.

She squawks at him loudly.

"Be quiet; you're fine," he says, and flips the shroud back down over her cage.

She grumbles in protest.

"Teacup," he says sharply.

Little Teacup goes quiet.

The Strelkie soldiers drag a screaming young man before the crowd. The leader yells, "It is illegal to worship any god but Ward Harrol. This building was closed for your own health and protection. Who knows the penalty for a secret meeting in a closed building?"

A Strelkie soldier shoots the young man dead. "He does, now. Is anyone else confused about King's Law? Or do we need to further educate you?"

The Punimin disband and head back to their homes, simmering. Three Punimin wail over the dead young man in the raging firelight. Elderman Hallow kneels with them to pray as embers and ashes from his church blow and swirl around him. Teacup peaks out of her cage through a split in the shroud and stares at the dead young man—and cries. Elderman Hallow will soon learn that flycubs are very emotional creatures, and more intelligent than most people he knows. But he doesn't notice that right now. Ejjer sprints deep into the woods. Elderman Hallow notices *that*, and decides that something about that boy bothers him.

A DANGEROUS ROOST

CHAPTER VII

E jjer hurries over uneven ground through the forest and trips in the dark. Though he's come out here many times, he's never come exactly this way—he varies his routes to avoid leaving a trail someone could find, and he doesn't use a lantern to avoid being seen.

His mind stings replaying the conversation his family just had with the Pistols. None of them know a thing about sprawhammid. Their silly ideas of rebellion, of love, of whatever they want? No, they can't just take a sacred word like that and carve it to their own liking. Sprawhammid means a God-given right to seize what belongs to you. That's what Ejjer has read in old books he's managed to steal from Strelkie who keep such contraband and treasures. It means destiny. That's so clear to him that when he first discovered it, he knew the word was built exactly for him, maybe more so for him than anyone else who has ever lived. Few people have a destiny as big as Ejjer's, this he knows in his heart. The word might have first been penned long ago in the Fourth

Age, and it has suffered with misuse over the crooked tongues of imbeciles for generations, but now it has finally wound through time and found its true and forever resting place: Ejjer. Ejjer is going to seize what belongs to him. He has it all worked out. And it is a glorious sprawhammid. Once he's finished with his work, no one will ever be able to use the word unless speaking of Ejjer.

A cruel upturned root finds his toes and he tumbles down a hillside, flailing. He lands in an ugly fall—near a large, empty nest. His accident couldn't be more unfortunate: a shadowy beast growls at him from the dark with glowing eyes. He knows it's a wilderucker. Ejjer almost soils himself but manages to scramble away from the place on hands and feet.

He ties Rose's friendship bracelet around a nearby tree branch, gives a good "memory marking" look around, and hurries off to where he was going. His target is elsewhere in the forest: his little "roost." A tent and campsite hidden among brush. Ejjer greets a horse waiting for him, then checks several crude hatches in the earth: this doored pocket has weapons, that one jewelry, this one Strelkie clothing. The spiders and gnats are easily brushed aside. There aren't many to begin with, not after he stopped leaving sweets and cakes here. That didn't work at all.

He slips on a Strelkie suit, adorns himself with Strelkie jewels, fastens a little gun to his hip, and wears a small fancy hat. He must think he looks like a member of high society. He rides his horse away and finds a trotting path. He rides it for over an hour ...

Until he comes to the walls of Strelkie City. The city isn't round, symmetrical, or even—years of architectural spats have made the barrier between "civilization" and "unwashed forest folk" jagged, revamped, and crooked. This rarely traveled area is a reservoir that was turned into a septic runoff into the forest. He once heard that two people—were they lovers, journalists?—were thrown off that wall—but survived, though he doesn't believe survival from that height is possible.

Behind its great concrete wall gleams Strelkie City in all its shimmering, vibrant glory. Ejjer hitches his horse to a crude parking spike, then sneaks himself along a fallen tree above the refuse and into the wall through a dry, broken hatch in the spillway.

He crawls into the bottom of an elevator shaft. A rusty ladder leads up and past an elevator hanging high above. He climbs.

And he soon finds himself walking out of a maintenance hallway, into a grand courtyard, one of many in Strelkie City. This is one of Ejjer's regular routes. Every time he feels like a caveman seeing a lightbulb for the first time.

There aren't any cabins here. No one goes to bed early so they can get up before the sun for their only chance to catch and cook a breakfast. People just wave their hands and food speeds to them on flying plates held by buzzing balloons.

There are *sidewalks*. Not mud, not cobblestone—sidewalks of polished stone. These footways are clean, and many of them ribbed with lights both day and night with traffic commands that change often but are easy to read. All the buildings are glass or gold or silver or stone, or twists and combinations. There is a repetitive elegance to it all. Whereas in Punimin country, houses leak and squat under trees and fear lightning, but the homes here are all apartments nested in high perches on buildings that seem impenetrable to nature itself. Clouds and moisture bring mold to the Punimin homes; here the clouds travel *around* the buildings. Perhaps they do so out of respect. The city is tall and bright and beautiful and pristine. To Ejjer, it's superior to anything nature could ever do.

The streets are for walking to and from work and parks and entertainment venues. Some vehicles ferry people to and fro, all powered by steam, and there are bicycles of every manner and size, from one wheel to six, from crouched to stilt-wheeled, and even some of *them* are powered by steam. Giant balloons carry anyone who wants to pass between buildings without walking. These balloons hold carriages on their bellies and glide effortlessly between palace tops, and they serve chocolates and cheese.

Machines roll and wheel and thudder-walk and crawl all over the place—instead of Punimin sweating and cursing and hammering upon all things, swift mechanical creatures do all the work, and the people are free to enjoy themselves and each other. (Never mind the Punimin servants scurrying like worker bees, and not a few Strelkie, who are often off in some corner trying to *mend* these constantly breaking mechanical creatures, many of which seem to exist only to drive the would-be repairers mad.) There is nary a bedroom window that isn't closed for romantic privacy, or open to dispel privacy over the same, welcome, concerns. Everyone here has a physical relationship and everyone knows it. It's in fact law that they do. No one is lonely, ever. At least, not by the narrowest definition of "lonely."

There are bright shops along the streets—careful, you need gloves to enter some of them, the kind that lock open so you can't steal—but that slight annoyance is worth the monthly charge to have access to the finest new gadgets available. There are holographic cards you can hold in your hand and use to talk to people who aren't even in the same room. There are glasses and goggles that show you answers to questions as you think of them. There are entertaining history classes you can slip into your brain with pills. There are funny little gizmos that help you not have to use your hands at all, small robots to cut your hair, wooden gum to straighten your teeth, candies to improve your bedtime rituals, and dreams sold in bottles to make anyone feel as they believe they ought to. All of this is available to any citizen because of the love and goodness of the king.

This is how steam power should be used—to create paradise cities. *This* is how talent and fashion and happiness should be distributed. This is how life could look and could be in the forest, if the Punimin weren't so set in their old-fashioned, backwards ways that fear all of this science and love. In Ejjer's mind, the Punimin are superstitious psychotics who would rather starve and live with stinking feet than know the supreme exhilarating thrill of a modern, joyful, peaceful life. Why must his family make everything so hard?

And the Strelkie don't know how good they have it here. Ejjer sees the ones who roll their eyes at the holo globe clocks from which the king's digital visage announces the time every hour. Do they not know what real tyranny is? Real tyranny is telling a young man he is free, but he spends all but two hours of his day toiling to survive, only to do it again the next day and the next. Some Strelkie fancy themselves philosophers and whisper that life would be better if they simply lived off the land and weren't distracted by all of the king's gifts. These people have never been farmers. They don't realize that tabled food is a luxury and they should sing the king's high praises for the rest of their lives and give him all the children he requests based on provided food alone, never mind everything else he gives them. Punimin live and die by the turns in the weather. To Strelkie, the king is the weather, and he is constant. Some Strelkie mistake this safety for boredom, they mistake boredom for misery, and they are miserable fools.

Yes, Ejjer hears whispers of discontent among some of the Strelkie as he passes through the city on his special trips. They ignore him, as he appears to be just another Punimin servant going about toilet management or something or other. But Ejjer hears. And he takes notes. And he keeps names. Because Strelkie society *could* be cleansed pure of these dissenters. And someday it will be. Someday, all things will be put in their proper place—first among them, Ejjer, if his plans come to fruition. And with every breath in his body, he swears they will.

Ejjer passes an execution platform in the public square—one of the smaller death stations. You can expect to see a Punimin at this one twice weekly having his or her body taken to pieces ("ripping"), which is good entertainment if you can score a smart standing place. Occasionally Strelkie find themselves there, too, for crimes and misdemeanors. Those are the best executions because they smell different—you can taste the fear in the air from the crowd when it's one of their own. And those are the times when the judges and head-snatchers get most creative. They love the show and the opportunity to surprise. Ejjer smiles thinking about the last one he saw.

Yes, Ejjer has plans. Many plans. They keep him occupied. He doesn't notice when he cuts through a side alley and marches right through a group of Strelkie whispering among themselves. He doesn't see them at all. Not the bright red hair of one of the women, nor the panicked expressions on the worried men. The faces of these folks look caught and trapped, and totally surprised when this boy, muttering to himself, completely ignores them and frets about his way—though he almost bumps right into one of them. They aren't robbers or any kind of proper criminals, but they have an astounded look at how close they've almost come to being discovered by an outsider. This is a close, conspiratorial gathering in what is supposed to be a quiet blind spot in a forgotten alley of the city. Whatever these citizens are plotting, if any servant can simply happen across them, they'll need to find a better place. Ejjer doesn't see them argue about this, he doesn't see them part ways, and he certainly doesn't see that some of them are quite famous, as far as Strelkie go. Two of them are assistants in government, and one is a lawyer of some repute named Toir Pat. Ejjer might have known that if his mind wasn't up his hindquarters instead of residing in his skull. But then, Ejjer's plans are the most important thing, and they only exist in his skull, after all. For now.

High in the city is one of many luxury apartments. Instead of dirt or wooden floors, this space is made of the finest steel, glass, gold, and tile. The air temperature is controlled. Nothing wild grows. There are no insects or animals. Plants are selected for decoration only and trimmed to geometrical shapes. Carpet actually exists here. And more than that—everything in here is designed to look as sterile and clean and safe as possible. Nothing is *carved*. There are no stranded splinters to find your feet and absolutely no competitive graffiti of tall tale stories to boast and lie about. Over a cold marble mantle hovers a holo globe marking the time, with the king's head smiling inside of it—no home is complete without its honor to the king.

The Strelkie have a *chief* emissary, Hollan Brattleback. This man takes himself and his appearance seriously. His nose is too big, but the rest of his face is defiantly perfect, and the disparity annoys him more than the nose itself. He'd rather be even and balanced. Right now, he's looking at his chiseled chin in a mirror as a striking woman, Carla Kutbee, dresses him. She's a beautiful but sad creature. Those happen to be her two most noticeable features, and Brattleback is mostly unaware of both of them. He and she wear similar outfits—all Strelkie citizens do. The powerful get medals or jewels to distinguish themselves. Fairness is their doctrine, but cheating it is their true religion.

The view outside is a haven of sparkling skyscrapers and lights. Blimps and balloons dot the sky and run in slow circles along endless invisible air pathways. It's beautiful, albeit sterile, out there. Like an aquarium.

It's strange to think this marvel exists surrounded by a medieval forest. The Strelkie pay extra for apartments with views that don't look out into those woods. They don't want to be reminded of how close they are to the wild. Everyone knows they could have been given to the Punimin at birth, and their lofty classism is a garter belt to keep each one's mind off that doom that almost was. To live as Punimin is to be wrong forever and never know it. If these Strelkie could see how much their tastes and styles, their steampunk sensibilities, matched the Punimin, they would be sick with identity crises. Their heads might explode like overwound watches. Everything, and everyone here, is wound tightly.

Brattleback notices lipstick on his collar. "Kutbee, you have to be careful. They'll put our heads on a pike. Or worse, exile us with the Punimin." He spits.

This isn't an affair with much love in it, and Kutbee has grown impatient. "No one will know it was me and not your current—"

He rubs at the lipstick mark. "This is your shade. I was caught with this shade seven months ago. Relationships terminate every three months. No cycle repeats. King's Law. Are you trying to get me killed?"

If she is, she won't admit it. "Of course not. I'm trying to make one decision for myself. Call me a treasoneer, but I like sex with whom I choose."

"You like political gossip," he sniffs.

"I'm a powerful woman." She thinks her answer suffices. "Tell me, is there a new law coming down next cycle?"

He smiles, won't tell. She scowls. A doorbell rings.

"Who is that?" He panics. "Your cycle child?"

She's caught off guard. "I have a teenager this round. It's a nightmare."

Brattleback checks a handheld palm computer-information-ticker, distracted, ingesting news out of habit. "My partner now, I think her name is Baxxy. Boxy? Something. The worst. *And* we have an infant. I can't wait for next cycle. I love Ward Harrol for keeping rotations short. If cycles were any longer, I swear I'd be a frog powder junkie." He snorts green powder from a small wallet-sized case.

"You *are* a frog powder junkie," she says dryly.

"No. This is frog powder mixed with snake powder. It's a new thing. Cleaner. Not for miserable junkies—I'm happy. I'm the chief emissary in charge of all Punimin. I have real status. People envy me." It's a lie. He's got deep pain, but appearances matter even in private.

"Of course. Live well, Chief Emissary."

"Live well, Kutbee." He kisses her cheek and heads out the backdoor.

She hurries to a bedroom: inside, a teenager plays a headset game with a helmet obscuring his eyes in a plain room. "Are you doing alright, kid?"

No response. She shuts the door. The doorbell strikes again. She runs and hits a keypad. A private elevator opens—Ejjer bounds in.

She's shocked. "Why are you here? I didn't order anything."

"I had to see you."

This is inappropriate. "But the front access? Ejjer, is your brain rotting?! You're lucky you're so beautiful." She kisses him—steps back. "You smell filthy."

"My key only turns on workdays. I had to sneak in through the spillway and climb up the elevator. There was a hatch. I took a stroll to air out. I think my walk did a good job of it."

She holds her nose. "A nice effort, but you failed. Shower."

He starts to undress and looks out over the city at night, which mesmerizes him. He has trouble with his uniform, and she helps him. Most Strelkie can dress and undress one-handed and in the dark. He looks the part, but his movements are all wrong and she enjoys that about him. Something human to counter his ungodly good looks. He wonders aloud, "I don't understand why Punimin hate Strelkie so much. You have it all. People should understand that."

Kutbee scoffs. "If by 'it all' you mean a junkie disaster. The overdoses are so high I heard Ward Harrol might have the border hospital nurses find fewer defects for a while just to boost our population."

"That would be a mistake. The Line works. It stays beautiful here. Pure, for the most part. Don't crowd it and ruin it. Things are just starting to get close to what they could be here."

Kutbee isn't happy in this place. "Everyone's the same. Every home is the same."

"But you didn't have to build these homes. Machines make everything for you." Ejjer is amazed every time he comes here.

"Machines make a lot of the *same* things. We can't have too many choices! Hurts unity." Kutbee just rips one of his stubborn buttons off because it won't come loose any other way.

"You don't want the 'choice' of living in a stick cabin or a straw hut. Trust me. It's so different here. None of your walls look like a child chewed on them. There aren't stupid pictures all over everything, ruining the designer's plans. Punimin are such scum cud."

"You're not."

He's undressed now, hops in the shower. She unearths a secret stash of liquor, her escape.

He yells from the manmade rain, "Can you put me in front of Hollan Brattleback?"

She almost drops her bottle at his audacity. "The chief emissary? Why?"

"You run the Credit Bank; I know you know him."

She's impatient. "I didn't ask how. I asked why."

"Because no Punimin sees what I can be. But you ... well, you almost do."

The backdoor opens and Brattleback sneaks in. "Sorry, Kutbee, I forgot my home key—" He hears the running water. Sees her guilty face.

Ejjer is oblivious. "My family is planning an illegal wedding and inviting all the Punimin they know. They're using it to build dissent among the people and start some momentum to rattle the king. I think it could spark a rebellion, or more." Ejjer turns off the water, towels up. "I'll give your chief emissary the details if he gives me a red voucher to meet the king." Ejjer pads out in his towel— screams at the sight of Brattleback and falls down sloppily.

Brattleback is not amused. "So, my side squeeze has a side squeeze. That's disheartening." He plucks the tiny gun off Ejjer's clothes pile. "Why do you want to meet the king?"

Ejjer is bold. "I believe he's the only person who can understand my vast potential and do something wise about it."

Brattleback chuckles. "A respected Strelkie and a stupid dirty Punimin. In your roost, Kutbee. You two carrying on is illegal."

"Are *you* two carrying on?" Ejjer demands.

Brattleback points the gun at Ejjer. Ejjer isn't scared. "If you don't have a way to dispose of my body, you're in for a barrel of woes. Also, I'm an errand servant; even if you turned me into ash, my disappearance would be noticed by extremely important people you can't afford to upset. Or are you above all reproach?"

Brattleback lowers the gun. Ejjer drips in his towel and says, "I volunteered for errands, and my family doesn't know. I'll volunteer to serve the king at the highest level, and my family won't know. I'm a great spy and I have strong Strelkie references." He gestures at Kutbee.

Brattleback scoffs.

Ejjer presses. "I have deep information on the Punimin. I know things even some border hospital nurses don't. I can be a favorite to the king—but only if I meet him."

Brattleback smiles. "You have big dreams, boy. A red voucher, if I give it to you, only gets you to the king's viceroy for five minutes."

"I only need four, sir. I'll give you my treasonists for that voucher. The wedding is in two weeks, or so."

"Who cares about one little wedding?" Brattleback asks.

Ejjer says, "Why did the Pirate Sisters first take to the seas in the Fourth Age and set fire to ten percent of the world's coastlines? Because one of their husbands kissed another woman. Why did we kill two Punimin clans in Almyter for failing to give up a baby? Because one misplaced adoption means the difference between the loyal friend or the cud liar standing next to you in the city. Why does the king hate marriage? Because love only comes from him, and perverting it into any other thing tears this beautiful country that we love apart into splinters. A wedding is a bastard's trick to make people think they remember better times, though there have never been better times than now. A wedding is a rallying cry to disobey and throw stones. Just one small stone, if lucky, can take the eye of a king. Even a god-king. There are Strelkie who want to see that happen. It cannot. And, my good sir Brattleback, this is not a *little* wedding. There is no *little* treason, no *little* betrayal, no *little* attempt to start a fire that *will* consume *everything* if it's given air. We must smother this now. Because otherwise it's going to be the biggest, damnedest, most inciting call to violence against civilization this Fifth Age has ever seen. People will copy it and quadruple it a hundred times over. The rebellions will grow and grow until a war is upon us and in every corner of every home and in every head on this continent. Then our foreign enemies will march on us with ease. But right now, this monster is in its egg, unhatched. I alone can help you stomp it out before it comes alive. I alone. So, unless you want this glorious, nearly perfect city to die and for it to all be your fault that it does, you have to ask yourself one question. 'What can I do for Clock Ejjer?'"

Brattleback considers this cocky rat. He asks Kutbee, "Do you like him?"

She nods. She knows the danger she's in and that she has to help Ejjer now. "He does what he promises. That's rare."

Brattleback looks at her sharply. "But do you like him?"

"Yes."

Brattleback shoots her in the leg. She wails and falls. Ejjer manages to keep his cool.

"Don't screw around on me with Punimin," Brattleback growls at her. "What's your name again, cud? Cog Wedger?"

"Clock Ejjer."

"Clock—" he laughs. "Okay, gizmo. Don't ever say 'treasonists' again; you sound like forest rot. I need the exact location and time of these *treasoneers'* wedding."

"You'll have it," Ejjer promises, "and the shared glory for rooting out their rebellion. King Harrol will love us *both*."

"Oh, us both? You know what?" Brattleback looks to Kutbee. "I like him, too. He does almost sound like a king. Almost." He sets Ejjer's gun down and walks past Kutbee on his way to the backdoor. "See you next week, squeeze. Same time."

Kutbee looks vicious but says nothing.

Brattleback sticks in the door and points at Ejjer. "I'm curious if this wedding can do all that you say. It does *seem* possible. But we won't let it get that far. We'll make something out of these rebels, to be sure. A good body count goes a long way with my friends to win favor. You may not be Strelkie, gizmo. But play your hand right, and the children you make could be. Just don't make them with her."

Ejjer nods. Brattleback leaves, softly singing the phrase "death to revolution" again and again.

Kutbee froths, "Ejjer, you *boff*-running, double *plick!* I hope a revolution *does* come, just so you can be buried in its ashes!"

"You used me for fun; I used you for power. That was glorious. Brattleback knows nothing of the real history of our times. How things work. How they spin on a single decision by the right person at the right time. But I do. I have ears to feed my brain, whereas he might as well be starving. I hooked that pathetic empty-skulled fool like a blood rat. He ate me up like dinner." Ejjer tugs on his pants and gathers his clothes. Kutbee winces as she gets to her feet and wraps a cloth around her bullet wound.

"Thanks for the shower," he says. "I'll deliver my information with your next scheduled errand. See that the chief emissary has my red voucher." Ejjer strides to the elevator and throws his jacket on. "I'll be kind to you when the king gives me a title and power. Probably." He puts on his stupid little hat and leaves—comes right back. "Kutbee, did you know that god-kings *decide* to be god-kings? I think they just know they're important. Do you think I would know that about myself? If I were *that* important?"

"I think you know everything, Ejjer."

He isn't sure if she's being sarcastic or not. But he's too obsessed with his own thoughts to care. This is the first time they've gotten to air out past the walls of his skull, and he likes the sounds they make. He walks out and the door shuts solidly behind him.

The cycle teenager shuffles out. Kutbee sits down and nips at her booze. They have zero relationship, but plenty of apathy. "Is the other adult here?" the kid asks.

"No. Out. Who knows where?" She's in pain.

"Yeah, so, do you care if I skip my lessons? Some friends caught a nosy Punimin and we want to do some stuff to him. I've never seen a lung before, so ..."

She can't believe this jerk. Concerned, she asks, "Well, have you done that before? Tampered with a Punimin?"

The teenager nods like it's nothing and produces a little glass box with a severed ear in it, a trophy from a heinous old deed. "There's absolutely *nothing* else to do, so ...."

"Come here."

He does. She cuts the palm of his hand with a knife and he recoils in shock. "If you get caught breaking any law, that reflects on me. Now you have to wear gloves. Leave no prints. And if anything you do *does* come back on me, I'll find some perfect pretty girl you wish to be in cycle with and I'll force her to chew off your fingers. Whatever jerk-sick things you've invented with your friends, I'll make them look small. I can outdo any teenager at any foul thing. Is that understood?"

"Yes, ma'am. I won't get caught."

"Alright. Live well, kid."

The teenager finds gloves, bounds away and mutters, "Cud" under his breath.

Kutbee doesn't care. She notices Ejjer left his tiny gun behind. She takes it. Happy evil thoughts cross her face. "Oh, Emissary," she whispers. "Oh, Emissary."

FURIOUS DESIGNS

CHAPTER VIII

The Pistols and Clocks are designing the biggest assault to Strelkie decency and law known to any legally published history since the rebellion that started the Greatest War one-hundred-and-twelve years ago: a big wedding. It is a glorious time for happy secrets and criminal pleasures. "Sprawhammid" is on everyone's lips.

Rose and Dancin fake their own deaths just as they planned (a hanged Strelkie woman for her, a wilderucker'd Strelkie man for him) and have the two bodies delivered to their emissary by friends, Iron Chester and Forge Wendy. They report to Rose that the emissary accepted the bodies without question, as the woman's corpse resembles Rose enough and the man is maimed well beyond recognition. It works just like it did with Net Nesting. It almost seems ... too easy. Rose and Dancin hope this ruse lasts, at least long enough that the wedding can happen without inter-ference and they can escape to Afar with their families as the guests return safely home.

While Rose and Dancin stay in the deep forest miles away from any Strelkie, all around the occupied village Punimin children gather pretty stones and stay away from the watchful eyes of bored Strelkie soldiers. These are their *wonderful crimes:*

Punimin maidens sneak loaves of bread under their dresses and skirts, past Strelkie soldiers to make *Prohibited Food.* Some of these maidens don't even know Rose and Dancin, but any excuse to make Barbellic cakes or Valorickan pies is worth the risk of getting caught. Punimin boys *Steal Strelkie Property* by yanking tips off a sleeping Strelkie soldier's wrap of spears, and dash away. Most parents allow their boys to cause trouble in the direction of Strelkie soldiers *if they're careful.* But oh, to be *encouraged* to do it —seldom do boys taste honor and pride so young. Getting to be naughty on behalf of their parents is such a reward that not one boy will complain about dressing up and behaving at the wedding to come. Allowing the boys to wear a piece of something they stole ensures that their vests will be ironed and their shoes polished. "Sprawahammid" is giggled through many children's whispers and laughs.

Punimin wives sew bridesmaids' gowns while hiding in a barn to *Recreate Banned Clothing.* Anything sensual, or remotely flattering, is forbidden by the Strelkie, and Punimin wives all have ideas about how they'd like to be seen. Some take matters to sultry extremes, which are reined in to meet a certain public acceptability by the eldest great grandmas—some by fewer degrees than others. Punimin husbands *Misappropriate Resources* and melt down the stolen spear tips in a small foundry hidden in a forest cave. The smell of molten metal reminds them of times when they were free to make whatever they wanted, untaxed and untallied by the king. And melting down anything owned by Strelkie is grand mischief.

Punimin grandmas shape the melted metal into invitations, or *Illicit Communications*. None of these contain dates or times. It's just a tradition for show—and clever grievances. Some fighty lady in the mix has a stamp that she uses to embed the invitations with clever slurs demeaning the king. She always wanted to be a poet, and is making the most of that dream now. When these people whisper "sprawhammid," it's not as naughty giggles like the children; it's more like a holiday greeting or a secret handshake, and all in joyful, if mischievous, fun.

Punimin granddads brew beer among many kegs. Hollers of *Illegal Drinks* are carefully crafted. The wedding is a great excuse to make too much. Pistols sharpen blades and *Stockpile Forbidden Weapons* like guns and war knives. This is supposed to be a safety precaution, but every secret smile and exchanged nod reveals an unspoken truth: they want a fight. When they whisper "sprawhammid," it sounds like a curse against their enemies.

Clocks Leslie and Zoe practice *Outlawed Music*, which is fast, frantic, and joyful. Leslie hasn't played it since she was a child, and it's been years since she's had something new to teach Zoe. Pistols Madrick and David lay out *Unlawful Tribal Costumes* and laugh together over secret plans. Madrick picks and chooses which cloths, buckles, and furs are sprawhammid enough to be included. Even with his constant laughter, he takes the sprawhammid word most seriously of all. It represents a high bar over which nothing substandard may pass. Madrick hasn't considered himself a spiritual man for many years, but something about measuring up to his idea of sprawhammid makes him feel, just a little, closer to some kind of energy that is larger than himself.

The participation of Rose and Dancin in this wedding seems to be the least of most people's concerns. Everyone who knows them loves them, they are a beautiful spark, but the momentum of this event doesn't want a spark. It wants a fire. It wants scalding hot freedom.

All of these crimes are crimes because the king fears they might otherwise catch on and proliferate. If they do, this is surely a wedding to start a war.

In the deep forest, Punimin teenagers lay out the children's pretty stones to form an aisle in the woods, through chairs and leading to an altar over which the Clock family (sans Dancin and Rollo) fusses.

This party is to be a private show of mutiny, a grand, thundering orchestration of sick contempt and rebellion that any Punimin would bleed to join. But not all Punimin are welcome.

Ejjer approaches the altar and interrupts his family's fussing. "Momma? Is there anything I can do?"

Leslie turns to him. "Well, you could see if the Pistols need any help with their business."

"I'd rather leave to gather more supplies. Rose should have roses. I know where they grow wild. She should know I can get anything—"

Clock Leslie pulls Ejjer aside. "Your brother is marrying Rose."

"I know that," Ejjer says. He tries to hide his feelings.

Leslie sees through him. "Quit being so friendly to her."

"But she's going to be family—"

"You're embarrassing us. Stop it."

"Momma, *Dancin is embarrassing us.* He could be a king's soldier! If we just make a few smart political moves, our family won't have to live in the guts of tree roots anymore. There are ways Punimin can live like Strelkie. Better, even."

She could almost smack him. "'Political moves?' You've never even *spoken* to a Strelkie, let alone a powerful one. And Punimin *are* better."

Ejjer fumes. "If you really think that then you should make Dancin join the army, because he was born of a Strelkie woman; he's not a real Punimin—"

She punches him square in the chest. Not hard, just enough to shock him. "Never say that. That's not how we are."

"No, but we could be." He wells up with tears despite his best effort not to. "The Clock family could rise to something better than this, Momma. I have a way. I have a very special plan."

"Do you know why you're the only one who doesn't know the wedding date? Because we don't know if we're letting you come yet."

He's gobsmacked.

"And," she fumes, "Rose and Dancin are dead, as far as the Strelkie are concerned, so none of what you're talking about matters anyway." She regrets telling him the moment she says it.

"You told the Strelkie they died? Why, because you think they won't find out about this wedding that way? They will. Trust me, they know everything."

"Forget I said it. Don't you *ever* talk about this, Ejjer. I mean it."

"You can't do that—lie to the Strelkie. Momma, that was so stupid. You have to tell them the truth. Maybe it's not too late. Maybe I can fix this—"

"No. Ejjer, you don't know any Strelkie! 'Political moves.' Stop dreaming."

"Stop stepping all over me! I have a plan for this family that will *work!*"

She ends this once and for all, she hopes. "Quit starting rotten arguments and fantasizing about living in other people's skins. It's dead ridiculous. And stop trying to impress Rose. Stop that right now, or you and I are going to have a very big problem. Do I make myself clear?"

Ejjer can't believe her. He storms away.

At the wedding perimeter, the Pistol family (sans Rose) works building a fort wall: sharpened logs like a fort-fence along a ditch. Clock Rollo is here.

Ejjer approaches but they don't acknowledge him.

Madrick asks, "How deep can a wilderucker tunnel? Did we put these deep enough?"

"It's not the tunneling," Rollo warns. "It's the jumping. This far out, where there's no people, they run free."

David assures them, "There'll be plenty of people."

Ejjer leaps in. "How will we keep the Strelkie out?"

They all notice Ejjer. David says, "Don't have to. They won't know we're here."

Rollo tries to dismiss Ejjer politely. "Son, why don't you see if Momma needs any help?"

Ejjer stalks away and runs into Clock Zoe dragging a sharpened log for the fence. He mutters, "You want to keep wilderuckers out, steal a baby one and tie it up far away. I could do it." He storms off. Zoe doesn't know what to make of that.

Beau asks the group, "What's wrong with Ejjer?"

Rollo confides in them, "I think he hates the king more than anybody and doesn't know how to deal with it. He'll grow out of it. Just keep working on this fence, now. Make it strong."

Ejjer boils with rage and storms along a ravine. A crow caws at him. He throws a stone at it and misses, but it flutters away.

This draws his gaze to a surprising place: he discovers Rose and Dancin kissing together by a big rock along the ravine's floor. He spies. This might go somewhere he'd love—and hate —to see.

SNAP—a wilderucker scratches a tree nearby like a cat stretching its muscles. It's a large, brown-haired yeti beast with thorny horns and chipped claws. Jowls with jagged, hooked teeth. Ghastly glinting eyes. Four hundred pounds, meaner than a bear, but not known for thinking. They're easily angered.

Ejjer picks up a stone and throws it—ducks—it clunks the wilderucker on the head. The thing snarls and looks around with dripping drool. Ejjer throws another stone toward Rose and Dancin. The wilderucker tracks it and lumbers that way.

Ejjer watches with suspenseful glee. The wilderucker suddenly roars and charges Rose and Dancin!

"Wilderucker!" Dancin shouts. "Run!"

Rose and Dancin leap up. She throws a spear at it, misses. She shoots a gun—misses.

The wilderucker goes for Dancin, who splits from Rose to draw it away.

Ejjer stomps his feet with excitement. "Yes, yes! *Perfect.*"

The wilderucker chases Dancin. Rose chases it with her spear. Ejjer follows. "Rose! I can save you! We'll climb up the ravine!"

She ignores Ejjer and throws her spear—it bounces off the wilderucker's hide, but the beast turns and charges back this way with huffs and snorts. Twigs and stones spew up from under its feet like skittering shrapnel. Its drool flies in every direction like heavy strands of broken spiderwebs.

"Rose, come with me!" Ejjer offers his hand.

Rose shoots the wilderucker several times—it tackles her. Dancin jumps on. Ejjer keeps his distance. Rose shoots the wilderucker twice in the head—and it collapses on her, still. Dancin pulls her out from under it. She's shaken, but okay.

Ejjer catches his breath. "Dancin, go for help. There might be more wilderuckers. I've got Rose."

Dancin fumes. "Ejjer, get Momma. The gunshots echoed; people won't know where to look for us, and there could be more wilderuckers nearby. Go tell Momma where we are."

Ejjer doesn't like the sound of her getting involved. "You know what? We're all okay. That wilderucker was a loner, I think. Momma doesn't have to—"

Dancin gets in his face. "Walk away now or I'll cut you, you *dagglehyde plick!*" Dancin's anger shocks Ejjer. He steps back. Dancin tends to Rose. "Did it bite you?"

"No." She's fine. Wipes off some of its drool, but her skin isn't broken. "You?"

"No, no bites ... so, we're alright."

She nods. "Comparatively, to it. Thank God."

"Thank God?" Ejjer asks.

Dancin and Rose start to walk away but Rose turns back and looks at Ejjer hard. "Did you get the wilderucker's attention on purpose?" she asks.

Ejjer is stunned. "No, I ..."

Dancin tells him, "I don't want you to come to the wedding anymore."

Ejjer can't believe it. "I was trying to save you. You thank God

—but what, you think *I* had nothing to do with it? It was me. *I* saved you, if you're really paying attention—"

Dancin simmers. "You sound like that damned Strelkie king. The only person you want to save is yourself—from this family! Well, that's fine by me. Go away." Dancin is a wall.

Ejjer shoves him—Rose instantly points a knife at Ejjer. "I liked you, Ejjer," she admits. "As a brother. If you ever want to be my brother again, I'll be here for you." She lowers her knife. "I hope you find what you want in this life. I really do."

Dancin takes Rose's hand and they stride away.

Ejjer storms through his normal walking route in Strelkie City, lost in his thoughts. He doesn't realize that a Strelkie woman has grabbed him by the arm and pulled him into an alley behind a buttercream shop until he's already standing there amid a mixed group of ten Strelkie citizens and Punimin servants. The Strelkie woman has confused him for someone else. "It's time. Where have you been?" She hands him a steam powered hand cannon with paper rolls stuffed in the muzzle.

Ejjer watches the group stare rapt at their variety of watches. The hands strike the hour at the exact same moment. Their gaze turns to the sky, where a passenger blimp floats between two skyscrapers. The Strelkie woman mutters. "Come on, it's time. Where is he—" Just then a Strelkie boy up in the blimp reaches out a window and dumps pamphlets from a sack like rain. Our clandestine group here shoots their small cannons and the same pamphlets blast into the sky, over the shop rooftops. The paper rolls open and fall like feather notes. The group howls and they all scatter their separate ways. Ejjer catches himself noticing one of them in particular, a woman Rose's age with red hair. He wonders why Strelkie citizens and Punimin servants would be playing a prank together. Ejjer doesn't understand. He drops the hand cannon they gave him and picks up a pamphlet. It reads: MAKE MARRIAGE LEGAL! SPRAWHAMMID! He crumples it up. This is bastard behavior. Sedition. And they're pirating his word! He must do something—perhaps get a clearer look at that red-haired woman and turn her in? A scream draws his attention to the sky: a Strelkie soldier throws the boy in the blimp out the window and he falls loudly to his death. The passengers on the blimp applaud and pat the soldier on his back. He is a hero.

Ejjer, on the other hand, isn't even seen. It's like he doesn't exist. He fumes with quiet rage. He's lost track of the conspirators. He thinks he sees the red hair of the woman Rose's age again, floating through a sea of people in a street like a bobbing glow of red down a river, but then she's gone, gone into memory.

Ejjer lies with his head on Kutbee's lap in her luxury apartment, a wreck. His contagious mood almost outweighs the beauty of the sprawling high-rise city out the window and makes the whole room feel grim. He complains, "This is the time to show the people King's Law is final. To silence the whisperers and crush the dissent. I can see *the moment* right in front of me. History is dancing on the palm of my hand, but I can't close my fingers

around it because my family is going to move the wedding location—they're going to move it, I just know it!"

Kutbee is thin on patience with him. She finishes examining
the hand cannon pamphlet-spreader he brought and sets it aside
like a useless thing. "You have to at least tell the chief emissary
when the wedding is."

"I don't know! The invitations don't say! You have to be told!
It's like they thought of everything!"

Doorbell. She shoves him and jumps to her feet. "Then make
up details. When you find out the truth, update your story—stop
crying. You wanted this."

He wipes his eyes and she hits a button: the elevator opens.
Brattleback enters. His clothes have been freshly pressed for the
upcoming occasion. Ejjer doesn't look well.

"Isn't he ready?" Brattleback asks.

Kutbee smiles. "Of course."

"I'm taking a huge risk, gizmo. Do not disappoint me." Brattleback pulls out a small glossy plastic card known as a red
voucher.

"No, sir," Ejjer says.

The viceroy, a hard-cut woman named Fillock Rampapart, lives in
the same exact luxury apartment design as Kutbee—only different
colors and a slightly different view of the city at night. All apartments in Strelkie City are essentially the same. Strangely, there is
no holo clock over the mantle here, no homage of praise to the

king. And the apartment is a pigsty with clothes and food strewn everywhere.

Viceroy Rampapart is an intimidating woman who finds herself wrestling with a little boy. Her current cycle partner, a frustrated man of little use, watches this, distraught.

"Help me put his shoes on!" Rampapart yells.

Her partner can't be bothered. "Deal with it. Last cycle, I had an amazing partner. This man, he'd always get the child to listen by—"

"Take him to the park." Rampapart offloads the little boy onto her partner. "And I don't want to see you for the rest of the cycle. My maid can't keep up with you. Go. Go!"

Her partner and child head to the door. The partner threatens, "No one's above King's Law. I could report this violation of unity to the king's chair-lords."

"I'm the viceroy, moron. I choose the chair-lords. Go, or I'll stuff you into a barrel of blood rats."

The partner and child leave. Sweet bliss. Rampapart collapses on her couch. Doorbell. She schleps to her feet, shoves some messy kids clothes under a couch, unlocks the elevator: Brattleback, Kutbee, and Ejjer enter.

"Come in, come in." Rampapart waves them in. "Excuse the mess. Bad cycle."

Ejjer is surprised by the room. "She has the same place as you."

"We all have the same place," Kutbee grouses.

Rampapart turns to Ejjer. "Let's have it, then."

Brattleback looks to Ejjer, who produces a red voucher. Rampapart recognizes it as one of Brattleback's. "Your last voucher this year, Chief Emissary. I hope he's good."

Ejjer jumps past social niceties and plunges into his plan. "I can give you the time and location of an illegal Punimin wedding, but I want an introduction to King Ward Harrol in exchange."

Rampapart laughs. "I thought you wanted to land some frog powder touched with snake powder. Isn't that what this is? Brattleback can't stop telling people about it."

"No," Ejjer says. "I don't care about that. I just want to meet the king."

Rampapart says matter-of-factly, "You don't meet the king. So, there's going to be a wedding?"

"Oh yes," Ejjer says. "It's dangerous, because it could lead to an uprising. It's like a dam—you don't want even one leak because the whole mess could burst—"

"Cud?"

"Yes, Viceroy?"

"Don't explain things to me; I know how things work. There can be no unauthorized wedding. Obviously. Where is it happening, exactly?"

Ejjer crosses his arms. "This isn't a small lawbreaking between two families. It's big. *Everyone* is coming, and they're coming to defy the king in every way imaginable. In the Fourth Age, splinter countries formed over less. This is the biggest rebellion in our time since Valoricka stormed the beaches of Army Bay one hundred and twenty-one years ago. I know exactly what kind of rare and important ground I'm standing on, and I need something in return for handing it to you in the precise moment you need it. History turns on gifts like mine."

Rampapart smiles. "You're still explaining things. Are you educated?"

"Early and often. I have good ears."

She muses, "Just good enough to be a knuckler. How about in

return for your information, I give you 'not being killed in the next ten seconds?' That's a big gift—ask anyone who knows me."

Ejjer shakes his head. "Make me your key assistant."

Rampapart smiles.

Kutbee can't take any more of this rude show. "Ejjer, just give the viceroy your information like we talked about." Kutbee absently touches Brattleback's fingers. She's a bundle of nerves.

Rampapart notices that touching like catching a poker tell. "Clock Ejjer, is it?"

He nods. "Ma'am."

"Well," Rampapart toys with them, "I like clocks. You can count on them. My inner circle is a trusted group. But I've found that Strelkie can be just as spurious as Punimin. Wouldn't you agree? Based on all of your education and savvy?"

Ejjer chooses his words carefully. "I would agree Punimin are cud and it takes a lot of effort for any Strelkie to sink to such depths."

Rampapart is impressed. "Aren't you political. Do you have any additional information that could sweeten the pot? Assistants really need to go above and beyond these days. And don't bother giving me more historical context to elucidate your mighty mental repertoire—I oversaw the chair-lords who edited the version of history I think you're citing. So, the only things you think you know that are of value to me are the things that exist in the present, or the very near future. Do you have anything like that, boy?"

Ejjer nods. "The chief emissary and Kutbee are carrying on outside of cycle."

Shock on the couple's faces. Rampapart nods. "You know what? I believe you."

Kutbee lashes out, "Ejjer, you bastard!" She shoves Ejjer and goes for the elevator—locked.

Brattleback betrays Kutbee. "Viceroy, she lured me! She's a whore and she drugged me!"

"Emissary," Kutbee says softly. Brattleback turns to Kutbee—she pulls the tiny gun she took and shoots him in the shoulder. He flees. Ejjer hides behind a couch.

Rampapart charges Kutbee—who shoots and misses. Rampapart easily disarms her, tosses her gun, and holds her in a headlock. Ejjer comes out of hiding.

"Everyone forgets I used to be a soldier," Rampapart says through clenched teeth. "Oh, this is the most fun I've had in *ages*. Clock boy? Gobble up that gun."

Ejjer picks up the gun and offers it to Rampapart.

"Demonstrate highest loyalty," Rampapart demands. "Do you know what that is?"

"Yes."

Kutbee yells, "He doesn't know where the wed—"

Ejjer shoots Kutbee in the leg—near where she was shot before. She may never recover, now. Rampapart drops Kutbee and lets her crawl out the backdoor and away. "Good, kid, but that wasn't *highest* loyalty." Rampapart takes the gun, empties the bullets, puts one back in and spins the cylinder of bullet chambers. Gives it to Ejjer. He hesitates. She doesn't like that. "If you want to be my assistant, hesitation isn't a word you know."

Ejjer puts the gun to his head and pulls the trigger—click. He lives. He doesn't look relieved—just serious. He knew he would live, because he believes his destiny is set.

"Oh, I like you," she says. "Now, the wedding. Every week

another rebellion is whispered about and I can't have anything like this happening to encourage them."

"Every week? The Punimin aren't that prolific—"

"No, Ejjer. The Strelkie. I have to keep adding chair-lords because power is the only thing left to give—people have everything else and quelling unrest is getting harder and harder. Two hundred years ago, Strelkie worried about wars. Today, they put the same angst into the speed at which their meals are delivered. Same anger, same whispers, same threats to those of us who actually have to work and rule. The better and more comfortable we make their lives, the more they find to complain about. Some people fill their chalice with fighting no matter the day. So, the last thing the people in this city need to see is the cavemen out there landing a shot across the king's nose. Revolution is sexy, even if you cut off heads in public to discourage it. No one realizes that after the revolt, after the lights turn out, it's back to the darker ages all over again. But if we can catch some barbaric Punimin in the act of defiance—and we punish them in front of the Strelkie, they hate Punimin and will cheer at their deaths, and by extension cheer at the death of revolution."

"But I've seen some Strelkie fraternizing with Punimin in the streets."

"We know about that, and it's being handled."

"Are you telling people that 'sprawhammid' has nothing to do with marriage?" he asks.

"We don't use Fourth Age slang here. We'll crush this limited defiance, and we'll stomp back those foolish city whispers about standing up against the king, the first king in two ages who loves his people. The minute you said the word, 'wedding,' I knew what was standing in my room. So, go ahead. Don't keep me waiting. Details, please."

"I don't know when and where it is. Yet. But I will. I swear."

Rampapart laughs. "Oh, my boy. You could be a useful assistant. You have courage for blood. But the brains? I can't decide if you remind me of the king, or one of my sloppier chair-lords. We'll see, *if* you can stop being a carver. Clean up this mess. Then get us something delicious to eat." She heads to her bedroom—

"I'd like one more thing."

Rampapart can't believe Ejjer's gumption. "Why on Earth are you still talking? You're the brashest boy in the Four Continents."

"If I deliver you the entire Pistol family, and my family, will you spare Pistol Rose?"

"For what reason?"

"Because ... well, I'd like her to be *my* assistant. Here, in the city."

Rampapart puts her hand on Ejjer's neck. "I'll think about it. Clean this. Get food. Now." Rampapart leaves Ejjer to it. As he cleans up the mess, he notices there is not a holo clock of the king in this apartment. There is no homage to him anywhere. He doesn't know what that says about Rampapart, and he wonders if sharing this information with the king when he meets him will be a wise move or not.

Later that night, Ejjer spends the better part of his time at home in his village, rocking himself to sleep in the dark, alone with just his nerves to keep himself company. He doesn't know how he's going to spoil this wedding and keep his promises to the viceroy. He doesn't know how he's going to achieve his destiny.

A MOST STORIED WEDDING

CHAPTER IX

I remember Toir Pat pacing before the jury in the Strelkie's dungeon of a courthouse. They are rapt, and so still that the creaky old box in which they sit doesn't make a sound. He tells them, "You can plan the perfect wedding. You can change the secret location a dozen times—and the Punimin did. They kept the Strelkie from finding out. So, what went wrong?"

The jury would like to know. And Toir Pat delivers. "Chance. You can't plan for what you don't expect." He points at the mystery prisoner in the box. "This one was undone by what Punimin call a 'terrible twist of chance.' What's worse than the bite of a wilderucker? Nothing but a dark secret spoiled."

Along the edge of a wide forest clearing once used to grow Punimin corn but now retired into a graveyard, a group of unlucky Strelkie soldiers are assigned to strange work at sunset. They dig up a wooden coffin, but as they pull it up with ropes, it slips and cracks open in the hole. A body tumbles loose. They look over the unsightly mess they've created.

Silo Countant, the boney emissary who disallowed Rose and Dancin's wedding, reviews a clipboard nearby and oversees, with two border hospital nurses who've been brought as medical consultants due to the health risks of the work here.

A brave Strelkie soldier apologizes, "Sir, another coffin split. We knuckled it."

"Stop doing that," Countant snips. "This cemetery was supposed to be moved already. The slower you work, the longer it takes to build the road, and the older we'll be before we know the sweet comfort of smooth carriages. I wish we were allowed to use balloons out here. But imagine if the Punimin caught on. They'd be in the skies. Oh, this whole country simply hurts my neck." Countant rubs his neck and it cracks.

The soldier feels compelled to share, "Sir? This is Net Nesting's grave."

Countant gestures to his clipboard. "I know, soldier. I don't care."

"But he was mauled by a wilderucker? Right?"

Countant is annoyed. "Isn't it obvious? The body has lost its constitution, but—"

"Sir, wilderuckers bite."

"Yes." Countant doesn't see where this is going.

"Their bites cause a disease that eats the flesh even long after you die. This should be down to the bone here and there, but it's all just ... regular."

Countant rubs his neck, worried. "Are you saying Net Nesting wasn't killed by a wilderucker?"

Viceroy Rampapart storms into her apartment and catches Ejjer by the throat. He's been cleaning the floor for her. "The Pistol family lied! They murdered Net Nesting! My cousin by decree!"

Ejjer blabs, "I didn't know that! Talk to *them!*"

"The Pistols and Clocks and their entire village cleared out! I'm told there's a hunting holiday? Soldiers at Fort Mary are interviewing Punimin in the ranges, but they don't know anything. Fort Favor is grilling the Punimin of the wood dunes who know less than that. I sent an envoy to the Punimin peninsulas, but her horse came back alone. And your wilderness seems all but *empty!* We don't have any Punimin to interview about anything until they come back!" Rampapart is a portrait of rage.

Ejjer mumbles, "How did my people slip away from all the Strelkie soldiers? My village is occupied. Many of the wilderness villages are."

Rampapart lets Ejjer's throat go. "The Strelkie soldiers are out relocating a massive cemetery. It was announced months ago. They're not due back in your villages for a quarter moon—but this changes everything. Where is the wedding?"

"Somewhere in the deep forest! I don't know!"

Rampapart would kill him if she could stand to waste the energy. "The deep forest? So, it's 'outside.' How specific. When? It must be soon—tonight?"

Ejjer stammers. "I don't—I'm trying, Viceroy."

Rampapart knees him in the stomach and he drops to the floor. She paces. "I'm sending the army to scour the forest. You'll join them. How it works is if you find the wedding first, I'll let you lick my boots. That will be the height of your existence until I like you again, if I ever do. But if you're not the one who finds them, boy, I will knuckle you, I will wash your skull, I will invent something to inflict upon you that will make even the most showy torturers shudder and weep. Every Strelkie babe will think of your mangled face anytime they look at a Punimin servant. Any body found in the street or tortured into rot that people see will make them whisper, 'poor soul, but at least they aren't Ejjer.' Find. The. Wedding." She shoves him with her boot.

Ejjer catches his breath. "What will their punishment be? The wedding parties. Still a swift execution in the public square?"

"Swift? No." Rampapart stands over him. "And not just the two families. All the Punimin guests. Examples must be made for those who violate King's Law. You do realize a wedding is a *religious* assault against the god-king himself? These weddings keep the cultish lie of their competing Punimin god alive. That's heresy on top of everything else. We'll make an unforgettable history of them and secure a safe future for Strelkie—we'll call it 'The Viceroy's Promise.' I like that. I'll be in the books. This damned country will finally recognize me."

Ejjer looks scared. She tells him, "Find the Sergeant at Arms. Tell her I've made you an advanced scout." She places her booted foot on a silver table. "My boots await your successful return. Live well, Ejjer."

"Live well, Viceroy." Ejjer hurries away with his heart in his throat and his guts running circles.

Deep in the Punimin wilderness, a *new* wedding site has been arranged among the trees in a clearing by a roaring waterfall. The water's sound is so loud, the hope is it will cancel any voices and music that rise to a carrying level. Ejjer hasn't been here, and finding it now, at night, would be a tricky feat indeed. There are many rivers and waterfalls on the continent, but all Strelkie maps that Punimin spies have acquired—old maps that call this continent "The West," older maps that call it "Yungdon," newer maps that simply call the whole landmass "Strelkie City," and still newer maps that call it "Strelkiedom"—none agree on half of the waterways' placement, and this waterfall and river in particular is one of the ones that exists on no map at all. It was only just discovered recently by some of Madrick's friends on a hunting trip that went all but sideways.

Paper cube lights thread through trees over a flowerful, colorful homemade venue. Aisles of chairs rest before an altar of spiraling wood embedded with painted stones. Candles on small, anchored boats line the shore of the river by the waterfall and chuck and bob with the current.

Many Punimin guests wait and chatter, dressed in their finest as a string quartet plays next to a dance floor. People wear goggles on their top hats and bowler hats and feather crowns, fancy weapons dangle on their vests, laced story-telling ribbons flow over their dresses. Every boot is shined to a mirror, every clock is wound tightly—and amazingly synched for once! Leather gloves stitched with the names of relatives passed-on hang loosely from belts. Dead trees have become pillars, carved of course, with stories predicting many splendid adventures ahead for Rose and Dancin —fanciful stories these, adventures on the high seas, many children, naughty passionate moments that would have been better left private—but who can stop Granddad Wyatt once his fast-whittling knife starts chewing? No one says anything to him because the thundering waterfall makes everyone tense. Should they shout their conversations to be heard? Or whisper to respect the reason for the disguising noise?

Clock Zoe and Clock Leslie co-lead the quartet. It's all so peaceful and beautiful—but the air is also vibrating with tense energy. The wedding itself is one thing to carry in the mind, but this mass illegal gathering, this forbidden grand event of defiance, has made everyone so excited for so long, now that it's finally here the Punimin are nervous. This party tonight will surely be remembered in sculpted clocks for generations, and everyone knows it. It is rare that a single person realizes they're about to be part of a great historical event, rarer still that every soul involved does. Whether the king ever finds out about this or not doesn't matter to them. This will be the place to have been in Punimin lore for a generation or more. They haven't had something this large that was wholly theirs in so long, they almost don't know what to do. They are as players behind a curtain that's about to rise. The bride and groom are relaxed, by comparison.

Suddenly, the waterfall slows to a trickle, then stops completely. All eyes turn up the cliff to see—forty feet up stands a group of three old Punimin eldermen who look quite grizzly and bemused: Elderman Ruckus from the ranges, Elderman Chut from the wood dunes, and Edlerman Pandolin from the village of Gunloop in the peninsulas. Each has their own flycub on a leash, little five-pound kitten-sized lionesses with wings, either perched on a shoulder, slung in a chest backpack, or standing alongside. The baby cubs look as proud as their eldermen parents at the feat of stopping the waterfall; they seem to smile. "Now you can hear each other!" Edlerman Chut shouts. They've built a rudimentary dam and feel quite pleased about it. It's nice that at least representatives from the faraway Punimin regions have come, but the sudden silence they've engineered stuns and stills everyone, even the string quartet.

The Clocks and Pistols look nervous, exposed. Pistol Jennifer shouts, "To hell with it! There's no point if we can't enjoy it!" Clock Leslie nods and starts the quartet playing again. The guests shout and clap and break into eager, loud conversations with each other as if they're at a convention.

Dancin puts the finishing touches on his tuxedo with his groomsmen behind a tent, a half breastplate with stamped roses covering the front of one shoulder and his heart. His Granddad Wyatt fixes his bowtie. Getting to do this means a lot to Wyatt, and Dancin smiles at him. "Do you think we're deep enough out here that we won't be heard?" Dancin asks him.

Wyatt nods, "If a Strelkie wonders this far away from the city, that would surprise me. *We* almost didn't make it out this far. It's so untamed, I'll bet there are species of birds here that haven't seen people since before the continents drifted as the maps claim they have. We're a walk and a bit."

Dancin asks, "What are those flying cats the elderman brought?"

Wyatt watches two of the flycubs pattycake clawed paws at each other in a fight while the third tries to fly, but its elderman won't let her leash out very far. "They're rattle roars. They're good luck. There used to be many kings and monsters, they say, and experiments, and abominations. But someone had the good sense to domesticate rattle roars and turn them sweet. The eldermen want to bring them back, but they're having trouble finding any males to breed."

"An endangered species at a wedding is good luck?"

Wyatt points and steers Dancin's gaze to Elderman Hallow trying to have a conversation with the other eldermen, but his flycub Teacup keeps climbing his chest and licking his nose. All the eldermen look grumpy about their flycubs, but you'd have to kill those men to separate them from their adopted children-animals. "Rattle roars were created by madmen to kill. Now look; they're flying furballs who love their people. Anytime you pull light from darkness, something that shouldn't be, that's good luck. That's love. You and Rose, happening in times like this, that's why we celebrate. Flycubs remind the eldermen why we cele-brate. Most of what they get to do these days is funerals. A wedding is rarer than an endangered flycub. Those cats are hope for the future. They're like you."

Teacup gets loose of her leash and flies away from Elderman Hallow—he yells after her, and she swoops right at Dancin and lands on his shoulder. Dancin freezes, frightened of the little thing, that hisses and attempts to roar at him. She puts her front paws on his cheeks and glares into his eyes. "What do I do?" Dancin asks.

Wyatt holds out his finger like a perch and clucks at Teacup, but she just swats his hand away with her tail. Though her tail is the width of a man's pinky finger, it still manages to sting him.

Elderman Hallow trots up. "I'm so sorry. Teacup, on leash."

Teacup growls at Dancin.

"Teacup. On. Leash," Elderman Hallow orders.

Teacup suddenly, amazingly, smiles and meows like laughter. She rubs her whole body against Dancin's face, steals goggles off of his neck with her little mouth, then jumps onto Elderman Hallow's shoulder and purrs as he clips a leashed leather harness around her neck.

"Do you want your goggles back?" Elderman Hallow asks, but he can't free them from Teacup's mouth.

"She can keep them," Dancin says. "I wasn't going to wear them anyway."

Elderman Hallow nods and walks away. "Teacup, do you know the difference between 'endangered' and 'extinct?' One is you in about ten seconds if you don't behave."

She swats the back of his head with her tail.

Clock Rollo checks one of his watches, then another, and fusses about the time. Pistol Madrick passes the moment carving a tiny wooden statue of his late daughter Ann. He oils it with his own tears and places it on a chair like a toy to watch the ceremony. He clears up his eyes, then sips from a flask to harden his mood into a more controllable, appropriate joviality—but gets caught by his brother's wife Grace. He reluctantly hands over the contraband flask, then sneaks away—to a bundle of tribal costumes he's stashed in a hollowed-out stump. Gruff men join him to review secret plans and serious business. In any other setting they would look like plotting bandits or thieves, but their scheme is altogether something quite opposite this night—though no less serious than the work of bandits or thieves.

Clock Francine fixes a flower girl's dress, just so, while Pistol Beau trades smiles with a guest, a fine fellow.

Off at the quiet wedding perimeter, a well-made fence of sharpened logs has been dug-in and assembled. Here Pistol David checks on Punimin guards quietly standing watch for the night. A few of them puff smoke on weed pipes. They trade nods: all is well here. Pistol Jennifer comes to fetch her father. Her hair has been done up in complicated curls in an attractive nest holding a crown of tiny pistols. Could these small guns possibly even work? Anyone who knows Jennifer knows the answer to that question. The extra bullets make up her entire necklace. She drags her father to a group of upset musicians. "What's the problem?" David asks.

Jennifer explains, "The Clocks said they're doing *all* the music. But our band is taking over for the reception. That was the agreement."

"We came all the way from Almyter," groans a musician.

David assures them, "You're playing tonight."

"Dad," Jennifer warns, "Mom doesn't want a scene."

David smiles, "That's up to the Clocks, isn't it?"

Pistol Grace hurries over. "What are you doing, David? Come on!" She whisks away.

David nudges his daughter. "Go, Jennifer. I'll be right there."

Pistol Jennifer looks suspicious, but hurries off. Processional music starts. David sees his brother Madrick (wearing tribal gear) wave him over conspiratorially.

Meanwhile, the dam holding back the waterfall looks like it will hold. The three visiting eldermen have done fine a job of log-dragging and mud-wrangling, and are sharing a full holler to celebrate. They've only come to watch their friend Elderman Hallow run this rarest of weddings, curious like scouts at a science fair who hope to bring exciting news back home. They decide to stay up here to observe with their pet flycubs, rather than join the guests below. It's a good viewing spot, they're dirty from their dam work, they don't know any wilderness Punimin except for

Elderman Hallow, and the holler is hitting them fast enough that the walk down the cliff suddenly looks much different than it did when they scaled it half an hour ago. Also, their flycubs are napping in their arms and they don't want to disturb them.

Moments later, the main event begins. Groomsmen and bridesmaids walk down the aisle in pairs to the processional music. Clock Leslie and Clock Zoe are focused on playing with the quartet. Dancin waits at the altar with Elderman Jones Hallow, who looks particularly excited to be here. He hasn't gotten to wear his green-and-white robes in what feels like years. His flycub Teacup lounges at the foot of the altar with Dancin's stolen goggles sitting askew on top of her head, looking particularly oversized on her tiny body. Everyone enjoys the procession—next come the flower girls, who are just perfectly cute. And now ...

Everyone stands. Rose appears at the end of the aisle in a gorgeous, *sensual* wedding dress. Both mothers made it together by hand, as is the Punimin way. Rose's dress is white and shoulderless, with long tight weavings of lace sewn into images to depict her childhood of running with dogs and wrestling with wolves. She wears white marksmen gloves, and the wrists hold live bullets in case of trouble. The back is open two thirds down and the front plunges, yet her skin is hidden and teased by a bandolier that is stuffed with white roses—on top of bullets and blades. She has a modest white train embedded with shiny melted flakes of gold, but not real gold: these are tokens and debris stolen from Strelkie citizens and turned into tiny ornaments to look like doves and dogs. Stealing something and turning it into art that becomes part of a wedding dress is a high honor—many Punimin offered their hands at this, and *all* of them can find their place crammed in on the train. The rest of Rose's gown exists to facilitate dancing. As she walks, a high split reveals one nude leg at a time. A single white garter belt with a small caliber gun attached is visible with every other step. Her feet live in tiny treaded shoes appropriate for forest hiking, but painted white for the occasion. Her hair is done up like a warrior—pulled out of her face, but layered and curled and fretted on top to show a prowess of weaving skill. To crown it off, golden paint is scrawled on her cheeks and over her eyebrows to look like fire. Mesmerizing warpaint. She is beautiful, stunning, sexy, and intense. Ready for battle, and ready for a party. Dancin wipes away a tear, careful not to smudge the complementing golden warpaint on his face. (Punimin dress competitively at parties, and the custom from many generations ago dictates that the bride and groom wear somewhat matching warpaint to distinguish themselves from all other guests, who wear nothing of the sort. People are still expected to not outdo the bride's gown, but on the off chance a wily aunt gets a showy bug up her craw, or an old wedding dress is the only nice garment someone's sister claims to own, the beautiful face designs limited to the bride and groom keep even the dimmest guests from being confused as to whose day, or night, this is.) Clock Leslie counts off for the quartet to start their Bridal Procession—but a MASSIVE DRUM beats from somewhere else and cuts them off before the first note. Teacup sits up straight at the altar to watch. The quartet is confused, doesn't play—

A little ring bearer boy, shirtless, in tribal gear, jumps into the aisle with the rings on a pillow and rebel-yells. He has a skull brand burned on the back of one of his hands like everyone else, but where most of the guests have taken care to hide or diminish this brand, the boy has painted a larger version of this skull on his bare chest. David and Madrick, along with some other sporting men, bang drums and chant, bark, and bellow like a warrior Haka dance and join the boy in the aisle. They all have the skull brand painted on their chests or backs with pride—and Madrick has also had two special skull brand patches made and stitched onto his pants: one for each butt cheek.

They dance and drum and howl like barbarians. Rose almost dies laughing. Surprised. *Loves it.* Dancin grins. These tribal men cheer on the ring bearer as he dances down the aisle. All the guests clap in time. Rose jumps in front of the tribal men and tribal-dances with them down the aisle. It's a wild show.

Clock Leslie and her quartet are not pleased. The three gentlemen eldermen watching from up by the dammed waterfall laugh amongst themselves, and their three flycubs wake up and stretch. Elderman Chut looks to be having the most fun.

The Procession arrives at Dancin and Elderman Hallow, who seems giddy. He slips a glove off his hand and lets his skull brand show. Madrick nods at him in approval. Half of the crowd takes the que from Elderman Hallow and removes their gloves, and a few even hold their fists in the air, knuckles forward, to show their brands. Punimin pride. It stuns Elderman Hallow and brings a hush over the crowd, until every single guest holds up their branded hand, knuckles forward, like a salute. Even Pistol Grace. Rose and Dancin do the same. Without planning it, every Punimin here has just reclaimed that symbol and come together as one. Teacup looks around, and mimics, holding up one of her paws with a serious look on her face.

Despite all the smiles, and some tears, Elderman Hallow has a sudden dread creep up his spine. A skull isn't a *good* omen—let alone a crowd filled with them. But he swallows his worry and gently waves his hands for the ceremony to begin. The people's hands all fall, but the gloves stay off—and many will be left behind for good. Elderman Hallow nods at Pistol David to start:

David clears his throat. "I give you this—" He gets choked up. Madrick puts his hand on his brother's shoulder. David continues. "I give you this bride. If your life makes her happy, then man, you live. If it takes your death to protect her, then man, you die."

Clock Leslie stands. "I give you this groom with the same conditions. Raise your children with only the best of yourselves, and nothing of the worst."

All the parents say, "Such is the Punimin way."

All the guests respond, "Such is the Punimin way."

"Be seated," Elderman Hallow says. Clock Rollo trades a teary nod with Clock Leslie as all sit in a thundering of shifting chairs and groaning benches. Teacup leaps onto Elderman Hallow's shoulder and quietly sits and holds still. Then for a second or two, the only sound is the dripping from the makeshift dam. Elderman Hallow begins what he was brought here to do. "Whoo! What a night! I haven't done one of these since my first year as an elderman back in Bearfield. And I haven't seen this many of you at prayer *ever*. It's good to be here in God's free country, isn't it!"

"Hey Church, just do us a wedding and don't hog the time!" Madrick yells. The crowd laughs.

As Elderman Hallow bobs around on his stage, Teacup hangs on to his shoulder tightly, happy to belong and be on this ride. "I'll hog what I may, sir!" Elderman Hallow yells. "Before we begin, I wonder if all of you have heard the story of how *I* was almost married—"

"I'll come pray with you for a *month* if you get on with it." Madrick grumbles. "Come on, Church!"

Other's shout, "Hear, hear!"

Someone yells, "Sprawhammid!"

Elderman Hallow holds up his finger. "I've heard a lot of you saying that word. I understand it has come to mean a lot to many of you. Standing up to the king." Some faces beam at him. "Standing up for love." Other faces nod. "Getting what you want." Some faces look slightly ashamed. "I'm old enough to know that people will take the meaning they want and do what they want with it, regardless of the word. But. This word means the quest to find God. It doesn't mean rebellion, it doesn't mean war, it doesn't mean love. However, those are roads. And different roads can lead to the same place if you're mindful, though each road comes with different consequences. I pray that the sprawhammid you choose is a road that leads to God. And not back to yourself."

Teacup looks at Elderman Hallow thoughtfully, then turns and glares at the crowd like his little enforcer.

"Church," Madrick yells out. "I'll pray with you for *two* months if you get on with it already."

"Six months," Elderman Hallow retorts.

"Four, best and final!" Madrick shouts.

"Done!" Applause dances through the crowd. Teacup seems to smile. Elderman Hallow grins. "I told you I'd get him one day!" Madrick looks grumbly as folks smile and rib at him. Elderman Hallow clears his throat and puts his taunting showmanship aside for his serious work. His sudden shift of mood makes everyone feel electricity up their backs, even his friends atop the dam. Teacup dismounts Elderman Hallow's shoulder and fly-falls to the floor, then sits on top of his shoe to stay safely out from *under* foot. Her leash connects to his belt and wavers loosely. Elderman Hallow's next words are known by all, but haven't been heard in a long, long time. "You have gathered with me now to begin a new story ..." The three eldermen watching don't realize they're silently mouthing along with the words, rapt, not even blinking. Their flycubs stand still, serious.

Out and away along the wedding perimeter fence, the Punimin guards sip on flasks, puff their pipes, and chatter quietly. The wedding can't quite be seen or heard from here.

Meanwhile, deep in the forest, Ejjer hurries through the brush with a spear. He looks desperate. Behind him, Strelkie soldiers prowl, armed to the teeth.

Dancin and Rose put rings on each other's fingers at the same time. They fumble doing it and laugh.

Now that the serious work is through, Elderman Hallow hams up his moment back at the center of attention. "It's about this time the holy man often explains, with torturous length, why what we're doing here is important. The meaning of it all. I brought an old poem about the Punimin love of the forest and how we people are an awful lot like tree bees if you think about it —interesting stuff. I worked hard on it." He smiles at the pained look on the faces, then continues, "But I understand the beer is getting warm and we're under some pressure if we want to get through this evening in one piece, so with the power vested in me by the one true God, and not that shite king the Strelkie bow to downtown—"

"Hear, hear!" Madrick howls.

"I pronounce you wed!" Elderman Hallow yells. The three eldermen on the dam shout it with him, not realizing they're doing it. Cheers and applause erupt as Rose and Dancin kiss. The four flycubs jump up and down, dancing like miniature goats. "Ladies and Gentlemen," Elderman Hallow glows, "Pistol

Rose and Clock Dancin! May their hearts live forever and be storied!"

All respond, "Storied forever!"

Elderman Hallow wants to make a further point, and a serious one at that. "Now everyone, we all know the risk of being here—"

A guest interrupts. "They couldn't find us with a map drawn on the king's ass!" Laughter from every corner.

Elderman Hallow nods. "So, for those of you who choose to stay—let the party begin! AND TO HELL WITH THE STRELKIE!"

Whoops and shouts of "sprawhammid" explode. Elderman Hallow shakes his head fussily at them, then waves them off and laughs despite himself. The quartet starts a tango. Everyone makes way as Rose and Dancin take the dance floor together for their first dance. The tribal men clear wedding gifts to make room for their "important stuff"—hollers of brew.

And Ejjer keeps desperately on through the forest.

Rose and Dancin begin a feisty tango, but the gruff musicians break in like musical commentary—they don't want a tango. Clock Leslie hisses at them.

They smile back like jackasses.

The quartet keeps playing and the gruff musicians "accompany," in their own way. Their battling styles play surprisingly well; Rose and Dancin dance all the harder. It's exciting.

And Ejjer makes progress ahead of the Strelkie soldiers. He must find the wedding place first.

Clock Zoe smiles playing along and stands. The gruff musicians salute her by holding up beers. Zoe quickens the song, and it becomes a tune they all know. The gruff musician's band leader sings. Rose and Dancin improvise their dance moves; all the musicians sync up and enjoy their fresh-harmonied creation. Glorious, frantic, exhilarating!

Ejjer is running alone now, the Strelkie soldiers so far behind him only glimmers of their armor in the moonlight give them away.

The song comes around back to where it started and ends beautifully, softly—as a proper tango does. Rose and Dancin kiss in a tight embrace. Everyone cheers. The gruff musicians bow to the quartet. Clock Leslie waves her quartet to stand, and they bow back.

Pistol Beau leaps onto the dance floor. "And all the people danced! Huzzah!" He starts a bonkers dance without music. The gruff musicians begin a loud knee-slapper to go with him. Everyone dances.

Madrick storms out onto the dance floor and interrupts this. He shouts, "Favor, Favor!" and everyone stops, stilled and silent, like a threat has just been called, or a fight summoned, or a duel. Their faces all look excited as Madrick points his finger and spins around, stalking the crowd, hunting—until his finger lands pointing at his son, Beau. "You," Madrick says. "Do you accept?"

Everyone looks to Beau, who laughs. "Oh, I accept."

The gruff musicians play "Favor, Favor," a competitive dance. It is wild and loud, and Madrick and Beau both do the same hopping and stomping moves at the same time, but each with their own flare. The people all crowd around them, and they have dance moves, too, but more like a chorus supporting two battling soloists—they compliment the competitive dancers. They stomp and they whistle and they sing and they shout, they pump their fists in the air and howl, and leaves on the trees seem to shake and the lights flicker with the throbbing spirit of their chants. The dance gains speed, faster and faster, with Madrick and Beau's feet tapping quicker and quicker on the floor, until Madrick finally gives in and falls down and Beau is declared the winner. Everyone applauds and shouts, and the musicians thankfully get to finish the song—the breakneck speed has scraped some of their fingers and winged some of their breathes. They wag their hands and crack their knuckles from the pain of playing "Favor, Favor" that long, but it's clearly not the kind of pain that a holler of drink can't remedy. Madrick picks Beau up and hugs him with a roaring laugh.

"I'm so proud of you!" Madrick yells. It hurts in Beau's ear, but he doesn't care. Madrick has held the title, undefeated, for as many years as anyone can remember, but now Beau gets to lead "Favor, "Favor" next time, and his pick his opponent.

The quartet takes the next song, a lively couple's dance that is plenty fast but not competitive, meant for everyone. Clock Rollo collects Clock Leslie to dance. She smiles a warm summer grin, ever in love. Everyone dances, from the little ones to the old ones and everyone in between.

What a party.

Along the wedding perimeter fence, Ejjer runs up to the Punimin guards. "What are you doing here, Ejjer?"

Ejjer catches his breath. "Get everybody out."

Pistol Madrick drinks and laughs large with Pistol David and his tribal men—and Elderman Hallow, with the three visiting eldermen who've now made it down the cliff—as the gruff musicians play on.

Teacup suddenly starts to squawk and panic, hearing something people can't, and the other three flycubs copy her in alarm. The eldermen don't know what's wrong with them and fret.

Meanwhile, Clock Wyatt and Clock Francine show off their old-fashioned dance. They're a little *naughty*, and if Francine weren't wearing skintight leather chainmail under her dress, she'd be more nude than the bride. They still have their old sensual moves. People laugh and enjoy the fun.

GUNFIRE. The party stops. Concern on every face ... David has a dark epiphany and shouts, "RUN!"

Strelkie soldiers leap out from every direction and attack. It's a mad raid. The Strelkie soldiers brought guns, spears, crossbows, and every manner of medieval weapon. They use them with prejudice.

Punimin fall right and left. The three visiting eldermen run and take their flycubs away. Rose looks raving mad. The gruff musicians start to pack up their gear in a hurry. It's chaos. Rose and Dancin herd the young children under a table. Strelkie soldiers yank Clock Wyatt's cane away and shove him over a table. Clock Rollo takes an arrow to the upper arm.

A Strelkie soldier yells to no one in particular, "So many pretty girls! Will no one dance with me?"

"We'll dance." It's Rose. She and her bridesmaids fight back overwhelmingly. They bust apart chairs and use them as clubs. Every one of them brought a knife, too. Vicious warriors.

Pistol Madrick, Pistol David, and their tribal men collect stashed weapons as Rose beats the lights out of three Strelkie soldiers. Four more hurry over and surround her. "Yield!" one of them shouts. "We've surrounded you!"

Rose scowls. "Your mistake." She takes them all on and beats and knifes them down so quickly that the last one standing ... just runs away.

Madrick, David, and their tribal men sprint onto the scene.

David throws a rifle to Dancin, who takes out a Strelkie soldier with a smokey BANG and a spray of cruel shrapnel that sends the pour soul quickly wailing to his death. Elderman Hallow disarms a Strelkie soldier and throws the man's ax into the head of another Strelkie—Beau snatches that ax free and throws it into *another* Strelkie. Somehow no one looks as ragingly mad as Beau. This isn't his wedding, but he's more offended and livid than any Punimin who perhaps ever lived.

Teacup bites her leash apart and flies away from Elderman Hallow. He yells after her, but she's in the trees. At least she's safe.

Clock Francine helps her husband Wyatt clammer to a relatively safe, out of the way spot near a tree. Then she lifts up her leg. "Faster, Wyatt! These motherless, godless fiends are quicker than we are!" He frees a whip from under her dress. She plucks a ball of nails from the top of her hair and screws this mace onto the tip of her whip. Her hair falls and she shakes it out, then kisses him. "Just like old times, right baby? Sprawhammid." She's nervous. He nods, scared. She hurries into the fight—

Someone tosses Clock Wyatt a gun and he uses it. Well.

Granddad Wyatt hasn't missed a target in his seventy-nine years. And all of that was just practice. Tonight, he is a sniping angel of death. Granddad lets no Strelkie who crosses his sights live. It's like his bullets have eyes.

Clock Francine whip-maces Strelkie soldiers. Rose shoots one going for a flower girl, breaks her gun in half over another Strelkie, and clubs both pieces of the gun against a third. She pulls two guns off a dead body and slides them to a hiding flower girl and the ring bearer. She instructs them, "Stay hidden. Shoot their feet. When they fall, shoot them in the face. Reload, repeat." The flower girl and ring bearer check to make sure their guns have ammo, then start shooting.

A Strelkie soldier rips an instrument away from a gruff musician and smashes it over his head. This is an unspeakable sin to all the musicians. Now they can't pack up and leave. The band leader sits down and mans the piano—machine guns pop out of a hidden compartment. The offending Strelkie soldier runs into the woods, to a group of his comrades—the band leader mows them all down. The bullet casings fall over her fingers and tinkle over the piano keys until the guns run dry. She looks at their strewn bodies with anger. "You don't knuckle the band."

The fight turns bad—four Strelkie soldiers shoot Clock Francine in the chest.

Granddad Wyatt screams, "No!" He limps to the Strelkie soldiers, shoots two, runs out of bullets. He beats one with his gun. They put spears through him from behind. Dirty cowards. He's come to his end and he knows it. But his last word hasn't been said. He rams himself forward into them like a porcupine— their spears are like fingers reaching out of his chest—and he uses their weapons against them. "Die, you damned Strelkie! Die!"

Pistol Jennifer tears a pipe off a Strelkie soldier's steam gun and douses him with his own hot steam. He calls her a "Punk!" and shoots her, a mortal wound to the chest that leaves her utterly shocked and gasping for air. Pistol Beau leaps in and cuts him down with two guns. Jennifer nods at Beau like she's okay. It's a lie, but he believes it. He moves on to fight someone else as she leans against a tree, stunned.

Rose gets cornered by nine Strelkie soldiers holding spears with moving chainsaw teeth. They carefully approach her. She knows she can take five of them, but the other four—suddenly a hiss of flame rakes across them and sets all nine on fire. Rose spots the fire's source—a flamethrower strapped on a female Strelkie soldier with red hair. Rose considers the woman a poor shot and herself lucky for it, and she runs to get into another part of the fight, not one to dance with that much fire.

"Rose, don't let them catch you!" the fire-spitter yells before she's attacked by Punimin with swinging swords and banging clubs. Rose doesn't hear her warning and doesn't really see her face. Not that she would recognize it anyway—she hasn't seen Lilly since they met once as children. Lilly ditches her flamethrower and sprints from the Punimin, into the forest to save herself.

Just then, the three visiting eldermen who appeared to run away shout from atop the dam—they're still here; they're prying their work loose with hard branches like crowbars. Their little flycubs swoop around like bats on leashes, squawking and yelling in a frenzy. The dam suddenly splits like rotten mush and a parade of water launches from the cliff, and pulverizes a group of Strelkie soldiers. The flooding rush takes Elderman Pandolin with it; he falls to an unknown fate amid splashy rocks, but his flycub breaks loose and flies away. A Strelkie archer takes out Elderman Ruckus with an arrow through the head. But the last one, Elderman Chut of the wood dunes, ducks the next flying arrows, snatches Elderman Ruckus' flycub, and races away with that flycub and his into the dark woods. He finds his horse parked with the other elderman's, mounts him, and makes like the wind with the two flycubs. The third flycub, Elderman Pandolin's, flies after him.

The flood is over in a moment, and it makes a huge mess of things, as to be expected from a brief tsunami. People scramble to fight through knee-deep pools and flopping fish that only make the shooting and stabbing harder. It's like a sloppy storm of fighting, one that Pistol Jennifer hardly notices behind her as her chest wound weeps. She takes her hair down and the small pistols fall out and clatter at her feet. A muddy flower girl, eyes blazing wild, scoops them up and gets back into the fight. Jennifer sits down, scared. She's bleeding out.

Madrick shouts to rally everyone he can, "Rendezvous! Rendezvous!"

The surviving Punimin scatter. This isn't a one-sided massacre —Strelkie soldier bodies are everywhere too, but their living still outnumber the Punimin, and they chase them in every direction. Pistol David pulls down a switch on a steam powered generator and kills the lights—darkness envelops everything. And the once-again roaring waterfall makes the dying screams of agony sound flattened and far away.

At a hidden shelter of branches and logs, their forest rendezvous, the surviving Punimin fighters gather more weapons. Who made it out of there? Pistols: David, Grace, Madrick, and Beau. Clocks: Rollo, Zoe, and Leslie. Elderman Hallow, and two tribal men. Some of them dripping with water, others dripping with sweat or the blood of fallen Strelkie.

Pistol Grace cries. "We lost Jennifer. She's gone."

David hugs her. Madrick straps knives to himself—he's all war-business, a cold butcher.

Clock Leslie reports, "We lost both my parents."

Clock Francine joins them—she's alive! And winded and

banged up. "Not me. But they got my husband. He wasn't wearing his armor vest because it hurt his back. I'm going to kill them all. Every god-king-worshipping, sack-of-frog-chewing *heathen.*" Francine frantically carves a knife into the back of her forearm, scratching in an image of Wyatt's face. She doesn't want to forget it.

Madrick gives her a serious look. "Francine, when this is over, I'd like to adopt you as my mother." He tosses her a curled metal barclaw invented to unhinge jawbones. She nods.

Clock Rollo asks, "Where are Dancin and Rose?"

Rose runs by with two long guns. Her mother yells after her, "Rose!"

Rose shouts, "They took Dancin!" She barrels away.

The group keeps arming up. Pistol Grace tells Clock Rollo, "Don't worry. We'll get Dancin back."

Madrick says, "Church, you don't have to join us. The *mean* part comes next."

Elderman Hallow insists. "It's not a marriage until the bride and groom make it safely home, and I promised you all a marriage."

Pistol Beau tosses Elderman Hallow a gun. "Is that a fact, Elderman?"

"It is now." Elderman Hallow cocks his gun.

"Good," Beau says.

Madrick takes charge. "Clocks, do what we tell you and you'll be more or less okay."

Rollo is scared but has hate in his blood tonight. "No mercy. Right?"

"That's damn right," Pistol Grace says.

Clock Leslie ties a bandana on her head. "Then let's go. This is war."

"This is sprawhammid," Grace says. She means it's more than war. No one disagrees.

The Pistols run with their weapons and the Clocks follow with theirs. The hunt is on. Elderman Hallow keeps Teacup in the back of his mind, and hopes that little girl cub made it to safety.

CHAPTER X

DEAD MAN'S RUN

The Strelkie warlords know not to travel at night in an enemy's forest. Years of mistakes in foreign territories have taught them this. The way back to the road is far, and the road itself that winds to the city from these woods is long and dangerous. They think their chances of getting home with their prisoner are better during the day. At the head of a winding dirt path just off the dirt road, Strelkie soldiers throw Dancin into a barred prison carriage. All the Strelkie soldiers left stand guard around it with torches. Every Strelkie believes the king built the city to protect them from the unknown terrors of the Punimin wilderness. And so they stew, and so they sweat, and so they wait to move Clock Dancin until sunrise. Ejjer watches the prisoner carriage, frightened, from a hiding place among trees. Now that he's gotten himself here, he's too frightened to move.

In the morning, the horse-drawn prison carriage and Strelkie soldiers march along the road. The Pistols stalk the Strelkie soldiers from the forest. They kept watch of the carriage overnight from hiding spots, slept in shifts, gathered their strength, and prepared for this morning. They like fighting in the sun, where mistakes are harder to make. They all wear warpaint now, as do the Clocks.

The Strelkie find themselves nervous on this morning, but have reason to believe in themselves. They have beaten the Valorickans in the North, the Barbellics in the East, and the wretched Wolf People across the Southern Fire Straits. They've even faced the deadly Pirate Sisters on several occasions and won as much as they've lost. Though never in all their slaughter and plunder, never in their trials of war, have they crossed a bride. Today, the Strelkie learn their lesson the hard way.

Rose looks particularly intense. Her wedding warpaint has changed and been added to—blood is paint-woven over her pretty gold markings.

The fight starts simply at first, quietly:

Madrick and David run out and club two Strelkie soldiers on the head, splitting their skulls, then disappear back into the trees like ghosts.

Strelkie soldiers shoot wildly into the forest. Madrick's voice echoes from somewhere, "Death to King's Law!"

The two tribal men who survived the raid run out and pick off two more Strelkie soldiers with daggers. An officer calls out, "Double time!" The carriage lurches forward with Strelkie soldiers hanging onto it on the top and sides. Dancin is manacled inside. The rest of the Strelkie soldiers run with the cart. If it goes any faster, they won't be able to keep up. They huff and puff and worry.

Rose watches from a position by trees with Elderman Hallow and the Clocks. She tears part of her dress off to keep her legs free. The dress's train is long gone. Blood spatters are all over the stories stitched onto her clothes. She's having a new story, told through blood. She orders, "We have to chase them now."

Elderman Hallow isn't sure. "But we planned an ambush. We thought they'd stand their ground. Chasing that cart is a dead man's run."

"No plan survives first contact with the enemy. That is our road. Now *run*." She sprints, and he follows her.

The hunt-and-pick-off-a-few-at-a-time game becomes an open foot chase on the dirt road. Who knew Clock Rollo was so fast—he gets ahead of the horses and waves them to stop, stalling the carriage—a brutal hand-to-hand skirmish breaks out between the Punimin and the Strelkie soldiers. Rose takes on five at once who wield large axes—an unfortunate error on her part. She has to duck, dodge, and scramble away.

Clock Rollo loses an eye to a dagger. Clock Leslie gets her arm badly broken by a mace. But Pistol Madrick and the two tribal men shoot dead three Strelkie soldiers. Clock Francine whip-slashes like a maniac—cuts down two ax-holding Strelkie soldiers chasing Rose and uses the barclaw Madrick gave her to separate a Strelkie's jaw, just as the tool was intended to do.

Rose grabs an ax and smashes the last three ax soldiers over a hill and yells, "Don't! Cross! Punimin!" Another piece of her dress falls off—the flowing bits have shredded away, and it's mostly battle garments that remain now. She doesn't have armor beyond some leather padding here and there, she's awfully exposed, but any man who thinks he might get close enough to cut her stomach or scratch a thigh probably has a bullet with his name on it. Rose is wigglier than a fox, fitter than a deer, and meaner than a wilderucker.

Pistol David and Elderman Hallow get pinned down and trapped by a boulder as Pistol Beau and Clocks Zoe, Rollo, and Leslie push over a dead tree—it crushes Strelkie soldiers and saves Pistol David and Elderman Hallow from them. The carriage takes off again. Five Strelkie soldiers cling to it with guns and knives. Pistols Madrick and Rose run for it and grab on as Strelkie soldiers shoot dead the two tribal men. Madrick swears under his breath.

On the moving carriage, Rose and Madrick fight their way onto the roof while ducking bullets and daggers. Madrick yells, "You should've put 'sprawhammid' on the wedding invitations! More people would've come!"

They tear through the first four Strelkie soldiers quickly and brutally. The last one almost knocks Madrick off—Rose catches him by the belt and kicks that Strelkie soldier onto the carriage driver—both men fall off and the horses run wild. The carriage barrels along harder.

Sudden doubt flickers across Madrick's face. "I know the plan was you get married and live happily ever after. But what now?"

Ahead—more Strelkie soldiers come running down the hill. They try to jump onto the carriage as it whizzes by, and fail. Rose says, "Still Plan A. It's just a longer plan now."

A jumping Strelkie soldier flies at Rose—she bashes him away. Madrick laughs. "I love weddings!"

From far behind—Elderman Hallow, Pistol Grace, and Pistol Beau snipe at the Strelkie soldiers. Madrick jumps into the driver's chair but can't reach the reins. They've fallen between the horses.

Rose shouts, "I'll get the reins!" But several Strelkie soldiers jump onto the carriage from a tall hill and fight Rose in hand-to-hand combat.

Madrick moves to help her, then sees a sharp curve in the road ahead. "Rose! Hold on!"

They take a hard turn. The carriage tips—Rose falls—grabs onto the side between wheels. The Strelkie soldiers on top of the cart shoot and jab at her. She tries to climb—gets hung up on her clothes. It's incredibly unfair. "You're lucky I'm still in a wedding dress." Her muscles tense like wood as she hangs on. She drips with sweat and other people's blood. The dress, what's left of it, will never be the same. But there aren't any Punimin alive today who wouldn't want to frame it over their hearth.

The road back-switches downhill in the opposite direction, approaches the road they just drove—where the Clocks wait. Rose climbs under the carriage. Now she's trapped over racing dirt and rock. Pistol Madrick jumps onto the horses and grabs the reins. The Strelkie soldiers shoot at him. That just makes Madrick more crazy. "Alright, then, you bastards. Faster! Yah!" He cracks the reins and the horses lurch faster. Half the Strelkie soldiers fall off. Madrick laughs. "Keep holding on, Rose! Rose?"

Under the carriage, Rose punches at the floor. Inside, Dancin kicks the floor. They're tearing it apart together. As they pass the Clocks, Zoe and Rollo jump onto the cart! Clock Francine manages to whip-drag a Strelkie soldier off from a place along the trail and kill him at her feet when he lands.

Madrick yells to the horses, "Slow, slow, slow! Whoa! Stop!" The horses don't slow. He yanks on the reins. "Horses, I'm talking to you! Whoa!" The horses ignore him.

Clock Zoe and Clock Rollo fight Strelkie soldiers on the cart roof as Rose and Dancin pull apart a hole in the floorboards. "Hey, husband!" she chimes.

He yells back, "Hey, wife!" Dancin climbs down through the hole. Now they're both under the carriage. Rose points a gun at the axel. "This is going to be rough. Uncle Madrick! Get ready to jump!"

Madrick glances at the wheels, sees a part of Rose and Dancin under there. He looks to Clock Zoe and Clock Rollo fighting the Strelkie soldiers on the cart roof—he clamors to them.

"Five! Four!" Rose calls out. The Strelkie soldiers hesitate. "Three," she shouts.

A Strelkie soldier wonders aloud, "What's she counting down to?"

Madrick yells and leaps at Clock Rollo and Clock Zoe.

"Two!" Rose shoots the axel and lets go—she and Dancin drop and slide roughly over the ground as the cart soars over them and breaks apart into aggressive splinters and spikes—Pistol Madrick grabs Clock Zoe and Clock Rollo and dives off the cart with them—they tumble messily as the cart flips and crashes into a group of Strelkie soldiers running this way. Bodies fly.

The dust settles.

Everyone takes a breath. Pistols (Rose, David, Grace, Madrick, Beau), Elderman Hallow, and Clocks (Dancin, Rollo, Zoe, Francine, and Leslie) trade hugs, kisses, and congratulatories.

Francine says, "We really should've put that on the invitations."

Madrick laughs heartily and hugs her. All the soldiers lie dead. The horses are fine and run away, free of the cart's shattered remains. Everyone watches the horses flee to freedom, and they wonder what that must be like for them. Then suddenly, Ejjer runs up to our group and yells, "You're alive!" But no one is happy to see him.

His father shouts, "Granddad Wyatt and Pistol Jennifer died because of you!" He slaps Ejjer.

"Papa, I didn't do this! I tried to warn the guards!" Ejjer shouts.

"You betrayed us! You're not my son!" Rollo has never been so livid.

"Papa, I know the viceroy. Rampapart. The king's right hand. If we give her the bride and groom, we can all be pardoned and live in the city like Strelkie! And that's just a first step. I have good plans. Papa, I know how to save us." Ejjer is desperate.

Pistol Beau steps forward. "You don't get it, do you? We will never be free in the Strelkie's world—"

David stops him. "Beau. Let them."

Clock Francine gets close to Ejjer. She tears a family clock off his clothes and stomps it apart into junk bits. "You're not a Clock. You're not a Punimin. You're just Ejjer, now." She pulls a small clock off her person, presses the clock face and a tiny little dagger pops out. She slices his cheek with it, and he gasps. There's more meaning to this cut than a simple wound, and he knows it.

Ejjer is horrified. "You can't take my name! That's MY NAME! If you leave for Afar—"

His mother Leslie hisses, "You never speak of that place again."

Ejjer backs up. "When you leave, my name is all I'll have. I'm going to rule this kingdom one day, and everyone will know the name Ejjer. I will be king. That is my destiny. That is my sprawhammid."

Rollo looks to Grace. She nods. Rollo says, sadly, "Maybe that will be your story. But not as *Clock* Ejjer."

Madrick senses something bold coming. "Hear, hear."

In turn, the Clocks each pull a watch off Ejjer's clothes. *He is shunned.* He doesn't resist, wants them to see his pain. He growls, "You can all die in the public square. I'll fix it so no one, no Punimin, no Strelkie, ever dares turn a frowning eye to the king again. I'll catch you and the people will love me. Ejjer the Catcher!"

His sister Zoe mumbles, "Good luck."

Ejjer looks stung and walks, then runs, then sprints away. He yells a wordless rage at the air, and is gone among the trees. Clock Leslie cries and Rollo hugs her, whispers something private to her.

Pistol Grace worries. "I don't like that Ejjer knows where we're going."

Clock Francine explains, "It doesn't matter. We killed enough Strelkie to make them cover the Four Known Continents looking for us. But Jungle Country isn't a Known Continent, is it?"

Pistol David answers. "No. My friends told us how to find Afar. The Pistols alone know the map coordinates and how to sail to avoid the boar kraken clusters. The Beast Sea is large and full of mysteries—would the king really risk his army just to punish us?"

"Let's hope not," Dancin says. "Were all of our provisions sacked at the wedding?"

Beau shrugs. "No way to know as long as we stay gabbing about it here."

Clock Leslie frets. "It's too dangerous to go back and look. Wilderuckers will be gnawing at the bodies by now." The thought of that brings a grim and bothered stillness to everyone.

Dancin hatches a fast plan. "Meet at the dock we set up by sundown. Go home and gather only what you need."

David suggests, "Bring gifts for the Jungle People. They're welcoming us into their home."

Elderman Hallow offers, "I have supplies in the crawlspace under the church—if they didn't burn with the rest of the building."

"I'll go with you," Rose says. "Everyone else, stay out of sight and stay together. No one wanders alone. We all leave for Afar together, tonight."

Rose, Dancin, and Elderman Hallow run one way, the Clocks another. Pistols Madrick, David, Grace, and Beau stay behind.

Madrick tells David, "I left some things at the wedding I want."

Grace nods. "So did I."

Beau suggests a wild idea they're already thinking. "The four of us can get in and out and make it to the dock before the rest of them."

Madrick, David, Grace, and Beau don't even need to talk about it. They quietly hurry away to dangerous business.

At the muddy and ravaged wedding site in the forest, two wilderuckers nose through the dead like vultures. Their wet snorts sound like warthogs. David, Beau, and Madrick sneak around and gather up rucksacks they've stashed. Grace takes a moment with Jennifer's body.

David whispers to Grace, "We have to go. The wilderuckers."

"I want to bury her somewhere safe." She looks fierce. David considers his daughter's body and is flooded with emotion. He was hoping the pressure of time could keep him from facing this right now, but it isn't so.

Madrick walks up to them with Clock Wyatt's body on his back. He taps them and points at Beau. They carefully put Jennifer's body on Beau's back and sneak away together. Thankfully, the wilderuckers don't notice.

At the Punimin village, no one is here. Those who left the wedding early or survived know better than to come back. Rose, Dancin, and Elderman Hallow approach a pile of burnt wood and ashes that were the church. There are wilderucker footprints in the dirt, but they could be old.

Elderman Hallow whispers, though no one is around. "There's a door in the floor to the crawlspace—"

A wilderucker jumps out of nowhere and grabs Elderman Hallow! Rose and Dancin shoot and stab it ... but it just won't die. They fire their weapons dry, and the wilderucker growls at them.

Suddenly, Teacup comes screeching out of the sky with her wings flapping, diving sloppily, and all four claws extended like little white needles. She's so tiny, but not too tiny to scare the wilderucker. She lands on its face and scratches at its eyes, bites an eyelid, and if ever an animal could curse, these are the sounds it would make. Teacup is fierce. Her attack gives Rose and Dancin time to reload.

"Flycub, move away!" Dancin shouts.

"Teacup!" Elderman Hallow shouts.

But Teacup isn't finished. She snatches one of the wilderucker's eyes, then flies crookedly away. Rose wonders if that little thing will learn to fly well; she's so floppy at it. But the thought is brief—Rose and Dancin put more bullets into the wilderucker until finally the thing stops breathing. But it's already too late. Elderman Hallow has been bitten on the shoulder near his neck. His wound is lousy with wilderucker drool. Teacup lands nearby and meows at him.

Rose and Dancin help him sit up. Somber looks all around. He ignores his mortal problem and casually gets back to business: "Now. As I was saying." He hefts open a burnt door in the floor. "Wine, water, and this month's financial contributions. There is also a pack of long rifles, but you didn't hear it from me. I keep more ready for trouble than my traveling eldermen friends. I'm sorry they didn't bring more people and I'm sorry they didn't fight. I should've invited their sisters."

Rose and Dancin fish out supplies. Elderman Hallow starts to fade. Dancin asks him, "Do you want us to stay with you?"

Elderman Hallow is a spirited man. "I'm not alone. I'm finishing my sprawhammid. I'll be sure to put in a good word for you with God. Go, now."

Rose lets a tear fall. "Thank you for marrying us."

"It was my pleasure. Thank you for letting me be a part of something. People will hear of what we've done. Just stay alive to make sure they do. And carve my adventure with enough exaggeration to make me proud."

"We will," Rose says. "We'll make you taller and everything."

He chuckles, kisses his hand and presses it to her cheek. He smiles. "May God bless you both."

"What about Teacup?" Rose asks.

"She needs to find a mate," Elderman Hallow says with regret.

Rose holds out her hand to Teacup, who sniffs her. Teacup looks back to Elderman Hallow.

"Go ahead," Elderman Hallow says. "Maybe there are flycubs in Afar. Go ahead, little love. I'm going with God now."

Teacup licks his nose, sheds a tear, then jumps onto Rose's shoulder. Rose kisses Elderman Hallow's hand goodbye.

Ejjer jumps out and shoots Dancin in the side. Teacup flies out of the way. Rose swings a blade at Ejjer—he blows snake powder in her face. The vile stuff was created as a drug for high society, but people have been finding more tactical applications recently, and Ejjer has long been among the first to lay hands on anything circulating the Strelkie black markets. He may know more about the various powers of snake powder than the viceroy herself. Rose staggers and can't see. Her eyes start to bleed, as Ejjer thought they would. He is proud of himself. "Ejjer the Catcher."

Teacup comes swooping and screeching—Ejjer swings a fist at her but misses. She wisely flaps out of the way and up into a tree, where she meows curses at him.

Elderman Hallow watches, hunched over, sick and dying. He glares at Ejjer in the distance, unable to call out, hoarse. Elderman Hallow notices a wilderucker wandering nearby. He clicks at it. It makes eye-contact with him. He nods hither.

Ejjer watches his brother suffer in pain. "Dancin, you're knuckled, now."

Dancin tries to get up—Ejjer pushes him down.

Rose staggers around, blind. "Ejjer, don't do this."

"When your sight returns," Ejjer says harshly, "you can either see my face, or the inside of a dungeon. Last chance to make the right decision."

Rose nods. "Dungeon." She comes blindly swinging for him. He dodges and trips her. She lands mouth-first in the dirt.

"Fine," Ejjer says. "I can have you either way, you know—"

A wilderucker runs at Ejjer. Ejjer shrieks and scampers. Elderman Hallow chuckles ... then pitches over slowly and dies.

Ejjer spins and blows his snake powder in the beast's face—it sneezes and staggers blind. Its eyes bleed. "Make some noise, Dancin. Maybe it'll find you." Ejjer laughs. "Goodbye, *Punimin.*"

The wilderucker howls like a wolf and stomps the ground like a bull. Ejjer wrestles Rose onto a stick with her arms stretched out to either side and ties her to it. He marches her away like a T.

Dancin lies quietly as the wilderucker tantrums; there's nothing else he can do.

Teacup watches from her tree branch, nervous.

The moon glows brightly over a western beach. The Pistols (David, Grace, Madrick, and Beau) and the Clocks (Rollo, Zoe, Francine, and Leslie) wait with Clock Jennifer and Clock Wyatt's wrapped bodies. The sea water is black-red and angry with tall waves. And to the north, something strange is happening: there are clouds on the horizon and they glow like they're pregnant with golden embers. The Pistols and Clocks have never seen anything like it; the closest thing to it was a forest fire twenty-two years ago, but this is different. It's as if the sky itself is boiling behind those clouds. It seems to them like watching a fireworks party from far over the horizon, except the fireworks are all the same golden color and bursting ever so slowly, almost out of time. It's quite a light show, giving an unnerving sense to this tense night and tricking the air into feeling electric and prickly with each breath the nose takes in. No one knows what it is, but when Clock Jennifer asks about it, Pistol Grace mutters about how it must be a freak storm somewhere over the Kings' Sea. Pistol David calls it a trick played by the moon when the light organizes just so on rare and hot occasions this time of year. Pistol Beau proclaims it is simply a bad omen, that nature itself is violently mad at the Strelkie. His words stick, and no one shares another thought on the matter.

Rollo is nervous with one of his watches. "They should've been here by now. We need to boat past West Death Outpost Island by sunrise or there's a high chance sailing Strelkie will spot us before we reach the ocean proper."

Dancin limps toward them, and Teacup trots alongside—they all run to meet him. "Ejjer ... took Rose."

"Took her where?" Pistol Grace asks. But Dancin passes out right there on the shore. Teacup meows and squawks, but no one knows what she's saying. Dancin's mother quickly tends to his gunshot wound on his side. The journey to Afar will have to wait.

CHAPTER
XI

TOIR PAT

I nside the grim courthouse tonight there is no jury, no judge—
just the prisoner awaiting the trial that will start tomorrow.
Waiting in her iron box. It is Rose, manacled and quiet. She's been
here for nine days. Thinking about Ann, and wondering if Ann
ever would've gotten this far if she'd decided to live and fight. She
wonders for countless hours if what she's done has been worth
anything at all, or if it all amounts to something worse than if she
had simply revisited that attic and allowed history to repeat itself.
Terrible thoughts choke her, and she fights back by imagining the
family she wants to create. She wants to escape and to survive for
them. For Dancin. For everything they may have ahead of them if
they can just break free of the Strelkie.

But such thoughts are worth even less than daydreams when
shackled in a tight iron box where there isn't much elbow room,
not for a body, not for a mind. The thin spaces that do exist are
meant for fear to fill, and how it does. Like water ruining a

canvass. Rose is afraid—more afraid than she's ever been in her whole life.

The strange lights in the sky stopped six days ago. Rose's last hope had begun to materialize as a hope that those lights were some kind of omen, perhaps in her favor. But now that they're gone, she wonders if there's any reason left to hope.

Then, the sound of a key feeling in a scratchy lock splits the dead air. Rose feels like she hasn't heard a sound for days.

A Strelkie soldier unlocks the heavy door to the room and lets Toir Pat in. He hasn't met Rose yet. He has the air of an aloof lawyer. Possibly hungover. He lightly, and not impolitely, raps on her cage. The silence of many days past makes that gentle rapping sound thunderous by comparison. "Are you ..." He checks his docket. "Rose Pistol?"

"Pistol Rose."

"Of course. You do it that way. I'm your lawyer, Pat Toir. Or Toir Pat, whichever you prefer."

"I prefer Toir Pat, I should think."

"As you would have it, Miss Rose. You don't have long to live, so however I can make you happy." He leans against her cold cage, tries to see her. "Can I get you anything? Other than food, water, and freedom?"

"Tell me what the charges are?" she asks.

Toir Pat chuckles. "What aren't the charges? Let's see here. Conspiracy to Wed, Conspiracy to Mutiny, Conspiracy to Rebellion—I feel like just 'Conspiracy' would have covered it, but they like to tack on. Killing seventy-three Strelkie soldiers—is that true?"

"No. That sounds low."

"Uh-huh. Committing Conspiracy to Sprawhammid?! Wow, I

haven't seen that word since I studied the *Holy Wars of the Sabban Peoples*. They're bringing out Forth Age conspiracy charges against you. You really upset the Strelkie. Impressive."

Rose shrugs.

He continues. "Also, you're charged with killing Net Nesting, a relative by decree of King Ward Harrol. Falsifying a corpse—several corpses—for purposes of, wait for it, Conspiracy—oh Great Ballad of Mordecai, there are ten more pages. Well, the good news is when the day finally comes, your trial will be swift."

"Aren't you supposed to defend me?" Rose can't believe this man is who she gets to have on her side.

"If I defend you in the literal sense of the word, I'll be on trial the next day. Plus, I have my reputation to consider. I'm the most well-regarded lawyer in the city. I had a somewhat famous, and somewhat infamous, grandmother who was well-regarded enough that people either enjoy my family name on their lips, or they hate it and praise me for outrunning its shadow. I do well either way; the word 'beloved' gets thrown around a lot. I don't want to rock that boat."

Rose nods. "So, not a fair trial."

"Strelkie justice isn't fair. I wouldn't pick it, but the overlords think it's efficient. Morons. The ancient philosophers would kill themselves over us." He hops up to sit on the judge's desk. "As long as the citizenry hears 'justice,' they go back to sleep. The last thing Ward Harrol wants is people waking up and thinking, 'Hey, life could be better without this god-king guy,' and rebelling. A loud wedding followed by louder fisticuffs is the last thing a man of my stature should consider defending and calling even more attention to. Unless, of course, I was interested in those rumored secret conspiracies going on—which

I'm not. Tell me, why did you do what you did? All this trouble?"

Rose looks through her bars and pierces her gaze right into his eyes. "This used to be a free country. We wanted to remember that."

Toir Pat shrugs. "I'm Strelkie, so I don't know what you're talking about. I officially gave up on all that a long time ago. *Not that I was ever involved with any underground groups*, mind you. No ma'am, not me. To me, freedom is just not getting killed."

"You have a low bar."

That strikes him. He hops down. "You sound like one of my friends. She met a Punimin up close once and said it was 'harrowing.' But I don't see 'harrowing.' I see 'troublesome.'"

"Trouble works for me."

"It works for you? You're going to be tried, tortured until you give up the secret location of Afar, and brutally killed like it's some kind of sport. If you don't spill every zig and zag it takes to navigate the Beast Sea without getting eaten alive, it's organs out for you. People will laugh and cheer when they see your insides."

Rose is caught off guard. "Wait—they want to know where Afar is?"

"The king wants to invade. Or his chair-lords do. Who knows these days?"

"What happens if the jury finds me innocent?"

Toir Pat glances at the door. No one seems to be listening ... He comes close and speaks softly. "Innocent of what, all the things you did?"

"Yes."

"Well, you'd walk free," he says. "That would make for quite a day."

"And what would happen to you?"

He glances at the door. Still no one there. "I'd have about twelve hours after that before they came up with something to charge me with." He looks to the door again—a red-haired Strelkie woman of around twenty years nods at him with fierce conspiracy, then slips away. Lilly. Toir Pat asks Rose, "Am I, uh, sensing those twelve hours would be enough time to hitch a ride with you and your friends to the Jungle People paradise?"

"Why would someone like you want to do something like that?"

"There's this old book from my grandmother I read from time to time that makes me think—it's not really important. Never mind that. Forget I said that. I need you to be completely honest with me, now. Are you the real deal? Because I was told you were, and I'm not sold yet. But I'd like to be." He looks grave.

"I'm just me."

"Don't carve me, kid. If there *were* underground groups like I mentioned not being a part of—which I'm not—they would, if they existed, hypothetically be *very* interested in a woman of your nature *if* she was the real deal. I'm talking you're not just a sassy forest princess who got mad that her big day got stepped on. I'm talking you're not just a wild maniac who likes to lick blood off of knives. I'm talking you're an honest-to-god—no, an honest-to-the-one-*true*-God *believer* in the power of the people and their sacred right to rule themselves free from an idiot king who ruins everything he touches, and his counsel of rotting powerbrokers who make him look decent by comparison. I'm talking you hate tyrants and believe in freedom. Real freedom, not safe freedom—dangerous, exquisite freedom. Do you *believe*, or are you just crazy wood snot? Because I am, hypothetically, interested in the very new and underground and secret business of raising up heroes. Heroes, not wood snot. It's vitally important that you understand the difference."

"I believe, as you say. Like any other Punimin."

"No, you're *not* like any other Punimin. You don't get to be, and that's the point. The wood dunes Punimin and the ranges Punimin and the peninsula Punimin are more concerned with the oceans that touch their lands than the city that controls your wilderness. Strelkie don't have the same grip on them as they do on your people—yet. But maybe you can wake them up before it's too late. Maybe you can rally the disaffected Strelkie, more importantly. You have a story, and bigger than that, *a torn wedding dress to prove it.* It's beautiful, and frightening—even though they took all your weapons off of it. You look tragic and heroic. I don't expect the judge is smart enough to order you into prison rags—they love showing Punimin as they are because they think you're disgusting. But that disgustingness, all that blood and mud ground into your neck and ears, that's *real.* I can see the freedom they took from you, that they would take or have taken from all of us. And you fought to keep it. You can inspire certain Strelkie among us to finally stand up and do something about all this stifling control we live under. You look like a person who breathes free air, even in chains. I can use that. You're who some of us want to be. All we need is a spark like you, someone who got hurt and wronged like you, someone to be mad for like you. And even though a Punimin isn't the best spark I can think of—a Strelkie would probably be better—this dress might make it work. You look victimized, but not *too* victimized. Wedding dresses are obviously illegal, so the tabooiness you have going on here is monstrously eye-catching. You're a wild combination. The more wild, the more fruitful. And the warrior sass, it's sexy, to be perfectly honest. That could bridge the Punimin-Strelkie divide just a *little*. Maybe that's enough. Maybe. Because I will tell you, people will want to be you or be wed to you. You're the ittest it I've ever seen. People will stand up for you like you're a damn rebellion flag. If I do my part. And especially if the scribes embellish a little bit and bustle you up for the record."

"You're quite a carver."

"When the spirit moves me, I can be."

She frowns, "But I don't understand the point of making Strelkie feel *anything* toward me."

"If we can get a Strelkie jury to say you're innocent, even though you're not, and if there's a way I can make that decision *mean* something—like a repudiation against Strelkie society—if we take you and turn you into the right spark at the right moment exactly, that just might be the excuse we need to finally get things moving along."

"Things ... like a revolution?" Rose loses herself in an unexpected memory: of the day Dancin proposed to her. His mention of revolution was a fantasy back then, but the prospect of their marriage felt almost possible. Now, a happy marriage seems a long way off, but the prospect of revolution feels like battlefield dirt on her fingertips just before dawn.

Toir Pat can't read her mind, but he can always sense when someone's guard loosens the slightest bit. He calls that "pouncing time." He gently brings her attention back to him. "Yes, as you say, things like revolution—and the end of this Age. The end of god-kings. Ideally. You never know which way the wind will blow after a fire starts, but you can shape certain parts of it. At least, that's what all the people in history who've tried to do such things imagined. Sometimes they were right, or lucky. Maybe the Strelkie will rise up and the Punimin will walk in step for a short time. So, what do you say? Do you want to be the face of my new good history, as I invent it? I can't promise you that anything painless or successful will happen."

"Well, seeing as I don't have any other plans at the moment ..."

"And if it goes side-bottom, I want a seat on a boat to Afar with whatever friends you have out there. Even if you die. I need safe passage and it needs to be a promise from you."

She blinks at him. "Is that the only way you'll invest in your revolution—if you have a backdoor out of it?"

"What good is it if we both die? You don't win revolutions by dying. You win by outliving the other side." He grins. Then he tears a piece of her dress off, folds it and stows it in his pocket. "A souvenir, if you don't mind."

"Until the part where you don't care if I live or die, it almost sounded like you wanted to be my friend."

"No," he says. "I want to be your and your entire family's most important friend ever. Tell me everything. I want to know all of you as well as I know myself. We have a spot of days before the trial, so give me your whole, full version of events, and we'll see if Toir Pat and Pistol Rose can't make a little history together."

"And a backup plan to get you to Afar in case you're not as talented as you suppose, and everything you try blows up in our faces." She smiles at him.

"Indeed. That is also important. Because whether you live or die, someone has to tell your tale. Your wedding isn't over yet; not until it starts a war."

CHAPTER
XII

THE TRIAL
OF THE BRIDE

The shafts from the courthouse dungeon's stained glass skylights dance on the prosecutor's shoulders and make him look angelic. It's a twisted irony; he is far from such. He leans by the jury with a confident, screwy smirk. Toir Pat stands by the cage that holds Rose. He is a helpless audience, but not without a strategy.

The prosecutor wraps up his case. "If Pistol Rose had been successful and gotten away with conspiracy, murder, and rebellion, then left to join the evil Jungle Country—a likely enemy of the king —what would happen to us next? What Punimin atrocities would find us in the next night? Yes, Punimin are just simple cuds—but they outnumber Strelkie."

The jury looks scared of that point. The prosecutor has them. "One wedding today, ten massacres tomorrow. As superior as Strelkie are, no one is immune to murderous poison. And Punimin are murderous poison."

The jury nods. The prosecutor brings it home. "Don't convict Pistol Rose because she killed a few soldiers, or had a little party. No, sentence her to death because she tried to end our way of life. Kill this snake in the shell. The prosecution rests." He shakes Toir Pat's hand like they're friends.

The judge rises from his perch. "Jury, this concludes arguments for the trial of the bride—"

"Your Honor?" Toir Pat stands. "May the defense speak?"

"The defense doesn't normally speak during closing remarks."

Toir Pat gathers courage from the red-headed woman jurist. "Yes," he says, "but Pistol Rose attempted to bring down our society, the god-king himself, and I am compelled to join the statement of the prosecution, for the record. Out of my devout love and respect for Ward Harrol."

The judge considers. "Very well."

The jury studies Toir Pat as he gathers his thoughts. "Imagine the world Pistol Rose tried to create. See it now. Punimin culture overrunning Strelkie culture. Free marriage, as opposed to our stable and dependable three-month structure. We get a new partner and child every ninety-day cycle. All love all. Punimin are tribalistic; they don't have unity. Punimin don't believe our king is a god. So, who makes the decisions in that world? Think on that ... Strelkie have one leader to follow. Punimin all make their own way. They think for themselves. How many people do you know who would be better off if they thought for themselves? Isn't that dangerous? Isn't that how carvers are borne to us? Isn't that how the Barbellics of the east became butchers and sacrificers and heathens? Barbarians don't believe in unity. Unity only works if every living soul complies and obeys, or is removed. We don't have room for barbarians in this uniquely civilized world. Scholars smarter than me would say our system is on trial. Our system is guilty. They would say that if you find Pistol Rose innocent, what you're really saying is Strelkie society *isn't the shining jewel we've been told it is since childhood, that Strelkie society needs to change. Finding Pistol Rose innocent of the things* we know she did *is an act of rebellion. You would be a part of something that would stand out in history forever. And given the attention of the trial of the bride, that would be a history so loud that every Strelkie would hear you. Every. One. History would know your names forever. Defense rests."*

Toir Pat takes his seat next to the bride's cage. The jury is a mess of frowns and thoughts deeper than they expected to endure. The red-headed woman jurist smiles at Toir Pat.

The judge does not.

The king's temple is the crown jewel of the city. Nested before shimmering, looming buildings behind it, it's a bulbous, round-topped globe mounted on a sharp pyramid with carved reliefs of historical events adorning every surface. Those reliefs almost make it Punimin, ironically, though no Strelkie would admit that. It's beautiful in some ways, but a mess to clean. Punimin workers who serve the Strelkie scrub it daily, and are at war with birds who crap their opinions of the king upon this place with hilarious frequency. The servants have been known to take their time, and no one who has ever been questioned has had any idea where all the bird seed comes from.

Ejjer strides across a large courtyard to this temple. He's in his finest Strelkie clothes and goes ignored by the citizens meandering about their day. He mounts the polished stone temple steps and opens a large steel door for himself. Inside, this place feels like a tall, giant mortuary. Large chamber doors with Strelkie guards before them remain closed.

Viceroy Rampapart and a small group of Strelkie soldiers and elite chair-lords drink champagne here and eagerly discuss matters of importance over a table displaying a layout of soldier weapons and snake powder that has been turned into paint. Rampapart ensures the group, "They're long plans, but they will work if we stick to what I've said. This country—" Rampapart senses Ejjer and throws a cloak over the table. She welcomes Ejjer, aglow. "Everyone, this is Ejjer the Catcher. He's the one who caught Pistol Rose and helped put that distracting business to rest. Ejjy, these are Ward Harrol's governing chair-lords."

Ejjer is nervous. "Am I going to meet the king now?"

The chair-lords' scoffs and sneers softly scream how inappropriate this request is. Rampapart shakes her head. "This is as close as you get. The king is busy in his chambers."

The guards eye Ejjer coldly. Rampapart pulls Ejjer's attention to her friends. "The chair-lords are the people I deal with. They're the most powerful Strelkie, save for our god-king. That's why you're here. They work so hard, I wanted to give them some entertainment."

Smiles on the chair-lord faces. Ejjer looks confused.

Rampapart boasts, with a hint of sarcasm, "Ejjer has great ambition. He wants to be king one day." The chair-lords laugh. "Oh, look, Ejjer." Rampapart holds back her own laughter. "The only people who could ever help you realize your dream just laughed at you. What was the deal we made? If you found the wedding, instead of torturing you, et cetera, I'd let you lick my boots?"

Ejjer wells up with tears. Rampapart's point for showing her friends Ejjer is suddenly clear. She wants, or needs, to look strong in front of them. Ejjer is just a cog to that end. Rampapart says, "This is as close as you'll *ever* get to the king, assistant." Rampapart knees Ejjer in the groin and he falls hard on his knees. The polished stone floor shoots darts through his nerves. The chair-lords laugh uproariously. Rampapart says, "My ambitious little pet here mistakes his jealousy for righteousness, like all low-thinkers do. He believes *wanting* power is the same as *deserving* it." The chair-lords stop laughing and look at Ejjer with bemused, mocking faces. He can barely stand the embarrassment; he'd rather die. Rampapart slides her booted foot forward. "Go ahead, Ejjer."

"She doesn't keep a clock of the king," Ejjer says. The chair-lords look bewildered. "She doesn't keep his clock in her home and it's the law that she does! Overthrow her!" They stand still, blinking. "Overthrow her!"

"Ejjer," Rampapart says softly, "we don't have to do what everyone else does. But, neither do you. You're the only person in the world who has the special privilege to lick my boots. Do it now."

Ejjer runs away, dripping tears. He feels like he's spent his whole life running away, and swears he'll have his revenge on them, on the world, on life itself. Rampapart and the chair-lords lose themselves in laughter as he flees. The guards quietly watch them with hateful eyes.

"Guards," Rampapart orders, "if he ever comes back, screw a spear through him, mouth to stern."

A chair-lord taunts her. "Viceroy, your boots look dull. How embarrassing for you to make an order but have it go disobeyed. What kind of country are we running?" Now the chair-lords turn their peevish smiles onto the viceroy.

Rampapart turns mad. "Guards, shine my boots."

The guards look confused. Rampapart feels the sharks all around her now. "I'm the viceroy, and you heard me." The guards hesitate.

Rampapart throws the cloak off the soldier weapons, plucks an arrow off the table, dips it in snake powder paint and flicks it at a solder—the tiniest droplet explodes and knocks him against the wall. The other soldiers get on the floor and rub her boots with their hands. The chair-lords whisper and laugh amongst themselves. "Use your face," she insists.

A guard whispers, "No."

Rampapart turns flush as the chair-lords keep chattering.

Outside the city walls, at the spillway, the Pistols (David, Grace, Madrick, and Beau) and the Clocks (Dancin, Rollo, Zoe, Francine, and Leslie) approach Ejjer's secret entrance wearing stolen, ravaged Strelkie soldier uniforms. They wouldn't pass a parade inspection, but they'll have to do.

In the dungeon courthouse, the jury enters from another room and returns to their seats. The judge, the two lawyers, and Rose watch them closely.

The judge seemingly has more important places to be. "You don't have to read all the charges; 'guilty' will suffice."

The lead jurist, the red-headed woman, stands. "On all charges we find Pistol Rose ... neither innocent nor guilty. The jury is split."

Rose is shocked. Toir Pat whispers to her, "Hung jury. Mistrial. They never redo a knuckled trial; you're free."

The judge and prosecutor look to Toir Pat. He throws his hands up like he had nothing to do with it. A guard unlocks the cage and lets Rose out. The judge is flustered and red-faced. "Counselors." The judge steps out. The prosecutor and Toir Pat obediently follow him to another room.

The red-headed woman approaches Rose with a smile. "Have a comfortable life, Punimin." She strings an old, familiar friendship bracelet around Rose's wrist. Lilly is all grown up since their meeting at the river long ago, and now Rose recognizes her—and suspects she saw her briefly at her wedding. "Maybe we're not so different after all," Lilly says. "I like to hope not."

Rose hugs her, shocked and happy to see her.

Lilly whispers, "I've thought about you every day since you saved my life."

"I don't know that I saved you; I threw you into a river."

"You changed me. I've done what I could for the Punimin, when I could. Sorry we couldn't get a unanimous 'not guilty' for you. For every rebel, there are ten counter-rebels. But we did better than those odds. I hope it's enough. Toir promised me he'd live up to my challenge."

"I'm just glad not to be dead," Rose whispers back. "Thank you."

The other jurists find their door locked.

"What's going on?" Rose has a bad feeling.

Guards wheel in eight large barrels. Rats squeal inside.

Lilly shrieks, "What is *that?*"

Rose knows. "Blood rats."

The judge returns. "Jurists, you will be put to death for conspiracy against King's Law. One bite kills you in two days with excruciating pain. We're going to find out what hundreds of bites do, in the interest of science."

Guards pry off the tops of the squealing barrels. The judge points at Rose. "You will give me the location of, and way to, Afar, in exchange for a quick and merciful death."

Rose shakes her head no. The judge expected as much. "Then accompany me to the public square."

Guards throw a net over Rose and drag her away. Other guards seize the jurists, who struggle—but there's no winning this fight. The guards force them, faces first, into the squealing barrels....

CHAPTER XIII

THE KING'S CLOCK

Guards march Rose along a ruddy old stone hallway with windows overlooking the city. They must be two stories up, following after the judge toward a skybridge to another, newer building. They pass Toir Pat and the prosecutor fighting clumsily with fists and feet against guards who mean to kill them. The guards stab the prosecutor. Toir Pat smashes a window, jumps into its frame, gives Rose a last, worried look, and flings himself out.

In the Punimin wilderness, Ejjer finds the tree he marked with Rose's friendship bracelet. He's close to the wilderucker nest upon which he stumbled. He wipes his eyes, mad at himself for still crying over what Viceroy Rampapart did to him in front of the chair-lords. He promises himself these will be the last tears he ever sheds.

Two wilderuckers sleep in their matted nest of packed brambles and stones with a baby wilderucker. Ejjer *carefully* steals the baby and sprints away.

Strelkie City's Public Square is a glamorously adorned but old-fashioned splay of cobblestone with an executioner's stage at its center. The red stains on the floorboards and cobble thereunder give away how well used it is. A large crowd of Strelkie have come to see a show today. Guards bring Rose, wrapped tightly in a net, to the stage. The judge stands proudly. He lives for these moments. Perhaps Elderman Hallow and he shared a father; in the bright sunlight the resemblance is similar to cousins, though this man has none of the departed Elderman Hallow's good nature. He's an opposite man. What life would he have had if the judge hadn't been sorted as a Strelkie on the Line? He never questions it. He yells, "Gather, gather, for the punishment of the bride, Pistol Rose!"

The crowd cheers. The Pistols and Clocks, in their stolen Strelkie soldier uniforms, are woven among them but they do not cheer. The judge unrolls an old map. "Rose, point where the Jungle Country is, and this ends quickly."

She struggles against her net and the guards. The judge presses her. "People will stop whispering about running away to this place if the king conquers it. This is the most important moment of your life—your last chance to do something good for the people." Then he whispers so only she can hear, "This is your last chance at a *true* sprawhammid. *Do something good.* Do something good for the people, Rose."

A nearby Strelkie soldier overhears and looks uneasy. The judge pokes Rose with a gnarled finger. "Where is it?" Her scowl gives away nothing. He hisses, "The pain will stop when you talk."

The guards remove the net. Rose thinks about Ann—or rather, how she would want Ann to see her in this moment. Rose yanks the net over the judge's head—guards pull her away. *Almost got him.* The crowd laughs. A few Strelkie soldiers posted around stifle smiles. Our Pistols and Clocks trade worried looks.

The judge mutters, "Knuckler," under his breath and straightens his robes. "Do you really think your disobedience will change anything?"

Rose looks wild. "Let's find out."

The judge grins at her insolence. "Percentages!"

The crowd roars. They were hoping for something like this. A hooded executioner wheels out a standing torture rack. It's like a table up on end with blender parts and grinding wheels. A steampunk nightmare-gadget invented with one purpose in mind: a clock to tear people.

The judge explains: "Rose, we will remove one percent of your body each time you refuse to answer a question. Where is Afar?"

Rose stammers. "East, past the Wilderucker Desert."

The judge can smell dishonesty. "A lie. Percentages double for lies."

The executioner straps Rose to the torture rack. The judge announces to the crowd, "We'll start with her feet!" The executioner clamps a crude device onto her right foot. It's a tube with rake teeth meant for peeling meat.

Rose notices a tiny shape flying high over the crowd, gliding smoothly—she's getting better at flying. Teacup is here.

Dancin looks to Pistol David, who looks to Pistol Madrick. Madrick nods: time to move. The Pistols and Clocks weave through the crowd toward the podium.

Toir Pat wears a cloak and follows them.

The judge smiles and yells, "Behold the price for conspiracy!"

Suddenly, Lilly battle-yells and runs into the area—bloody, rat-bitten, carrying two small storage barrels and a torch. A blood rat scrambles in her red hair. "Death to King's Law! Sprawhammid!"

Rose is reminded of seeing that red hair bob in the river when they were ten years old. Now it flies in the air like a defiant storm cloud, against the wind. If they had never met, Rose's life might have been much the same as it was. But Lilly's would not. She wouldn't have become a revolutionary, nor a lover of Punimin. And she would never have become a brave soul.

Lilly throws the small barrels under the stage. They leak black powder. She hurls her torch—a guard catches her and the torch flies askew. The guard stabs her. She rips her blood rat from her hair and jams the squealing, clambering little monster onto his neck—a Strelkie soldier shoots him *and* the blood rat.

Lilly smiles. "You're dead, now. Revolution. Sprawhammid." She dies with a firm smile on her face, like she knows something no one else does. The Strelkie soldiers have killed many people, but never seen a death face like that. Lilly has practiced this grin, meaning to die wearing it. She's rehearsed it ever since she first saw its mad liveliness on young Rose at the river that day when she took down two men three times her size. Lilly leaves life proud to have done something worthy of that mad expression, of that look of wild and earned righteousness. For a brief moment, her frozen face haunts the soldiers, and they feel worry like they never have before.

The judge is flustered beyond repair. "Where did she get that gunpowder?"

An unhappy guard who was put up to talking to the judge says, "The armory's next to the dungeon, sir. The lawyer, Toir, he pried it open."

"Find him."

The guard runs past our cloaked Toir Pat—*a gunpowder trail leads from under his cloak, to his feet, back the way he came.*

The judge collects what he can of his composure. "Executioner, please resume." The judge notices the crowd is frozen with shock. The judge turns—the executioner's head falls away from his body and he tumbles—revealing Pistol Madrick with a sword and a war grin.

The judge recoils, petrified. The Pistols and Clocks attack the guards. They look just like Strelkie soldiers doing it. The crowd panics. The real Strelkie soldiers don't know what to do, hesitate. The judge screams, "Soldiers! Kill them!"

Dancin unshackles and frees Rose from the torture rack, but can't get the last strap loose. Teacup lands—she's wearing a little leather battle vest and helmet—and bites the last strap free.

"Thanks, Teacup," Rose says. She beelines for the judge. He draws a gun on her—Clock Francine whip-cuts his hand off! Teacup flies and catches it, then drops it to Rose. She pulls the gun off the hand and blows the judge away with a shot right between the eyes.

Pistol Madrick presses Rose's forehead to his. He yells, war-drunk, "It's so beautiful, Rose! I love it! I LOVE IT!" He turns and fights in a blissful, brawling rage. He carries a metal stamp on steel knuckles—a new visage of Ann—and more Strelkie than Madrick counts die with her face dented into theirs. Madrick screams "sprawhammid" like a curse with every blow he delivers. He's in his prime and his war has finally come. He swings his sword so hard and fast that it whistles as it slices the air. It sounds like music to him. And the bodies that hit the floor are his drumbeat. Pistol Beau is at his side, full of frothy fire and ecstatic rage —like father, like son. Theirs is a dance to inspire the war poets.

Some Strelkie soldiers attack the families; some just watch and rethink their loyalties.

Rose slashes through Strelkie soldiers with all-out barbarism while Clocks Rollo and Leslie fight alongside Pistols Grace and David in a chaotic brawl. Teacup finds one face after another to scratch and bite. Clocks Zoe and Grandma Francine take out three Strelkie soldiers with swift, cold maneuvers dreamed up to sting them heartily as they die.

In the panic of soldiers scurrying every which way, Rose misses a marksman aiming a careful arrow at her. She's too busy cutting Strelkie down to notice the arrow fly after her—then she sees Ann, standing before her, almost as a ghost. She can't be real, can she be? Ann screams at Rose to lift up her hand to her side, and without thinking Rose does—

Rose catches an arrow in her fingers. She can't believe it— neither can the Strelkie soldier who shot at her: he smiles in amazement—she runs at him and stabs him with it and he squeals. Rose looks back to where Ann appeared a moment ago, but she's gone.

A wild fracas breaks out. The crowd has had enough of this show and flees—no they don't; hold on—Ejjer stands at the main gate with a convulsing sack. What does he have in there? Everyone who sees it hesitates at the sight of it. Ejjer opens the bag—the tiny baby wilderucker he stole. "Death to the king! Death to you all!" He runs into the crowd with the baby. Howls sound off—two wilderuckers *chase him and attack anyone who comes near.* Ejjer has put the crowd between a baby cub and two vicious parents. The crowd scatters and people ram into each other like mad as the Punimin families keep fighting the Strelkie soldiers on the platform.

Toir Pat fights alongside the Clocks, bleeding with them, in the thick of the fray. "Rose! Get off the platform!"

"Why would I do that?" Rose slams the torture rack onto a Strelkie soldier and it sets off like a dozen wicked mousetraps. Teacup swoops by screaming.

In the nearby armory, a candle burns a rope holding a bowl of burning wood over Toir Pat's trail of gunpowder. The rope will break soon.

But Rose doesn't know that. On the executioner's stage, she and Dancin throw a Strelkie soldier at a wilderucker in the scattering crowd below. The beast does more to that man in two seconds than the executioner could with a week. She sees Ejjer hurrying through the square.

"Rose!" Toir Pat yells. "It's going to blow!"

"What?" She can't hear him over all the panic and noise.

Toir Pat is trapped dueling a Strelkie soldier, but manages to shout at her, "We didn't want them to torture you!"

"So, you planned to blow me up?!" she yells. "You were going to martyr me?"

"Better than torture! But now I don't want you to die! I like you, kid! And martyrs are boring because they're dead! You stay alive, you stay interesting, and you help us kill our way all the way up to the king! It's war and the Fifth Age ends today!"

Great swells of battle cries sound from the horizon—you can see part of one of the tall outer city walls from here, though it's many blocks away. It's less guarded than usual because of the attention being paid to the executioner's platform. Ladders peek over the wall's top, and a roaring rush of Punimin come clamoring over—Punimin from the wood dunes, Punimin from the ranges, Punimin from the peninsulas, and ahead of them, one very angry elderman who waves a strange flag. It's Elderman Chut, who fled the wedding attack on a horse, and pinned to his flag proclaiming revolution is a scrap of Rose's wedding dress—the piece that Toir Pat snatched off of her.

Rose is shocked at the sight. "Did you do that? How did you do that?" she asks Toir Pat.

He admits, "I keep in touch with various people throughout the country by bird messengers. It's not that difficult—but everything that follows *will* be if you don't get off of there! I want to meet your family, and that'll be more pleasant if you're not in a thousand pieces!"

In the armory, the rope snaps; the fire bowl lands on the gunpowder. FLASH!

Dancin helps Clock Francine off the stage as Teacup screams with a baby war roar and zips through the air behind her, a blur of lioness and wings and leather armor. Toir Pat helps Rose down as the rest of her family keeps fighting and the invading Punimin clash with Strelkie soldiers.

Rose imagines seeing Ann pressing through the crowd with her, smiling at her. Rose doesn't know if this vision is real or a trick of her heart confused by the excitement, but she does know something for certain, to her core: on this day, Ann admires her. Ann is proud of her.

Rose spots Dancin as Clock Francine shakes him off to escape on her own two feet. "Dancin!" Rose calls. "Over here." Rose kisses Dancin, unaware as a fire trail rips along the gunpowder and hits the barrels Lilly dropped—BOOM! The entire platform explodes and sends everyone flying. The soldiers who witnessed Lilly's death grin learn in an instant what she was so happy about, but their faces do not match hers as they depart the world—they leave by weeping pieces.

In the armory, the fire bowl inadvertently sets the floor on fire like a liquor spill—it leads to a towering stockpile of gunpowder. When that heap blows, Strelkie and Punimin alike get hit—

The blast can be seen several blocks away, as far as the king's temple. The explosion shakes buildings and vibrates the city. Ejjer is here at the temple, holding his baby wilderucker in the outer keep, before those chamber doors the viceroy and chair-lords wouldn't let him pass through—the doors that keep King Ward Harrol safe from his people.

The two scared guards at these doors consider Ejjer carefully. Ejjer says, "Open the king's chambers."

The braver guard musters, "The viceroy and chair-lords are meeting with the king and we're under attack. We have orders to skewer you. Please just leave."

They want nothing to do with the little beast in Ejjer's arms, or the monster family that's coming for it. Ejjer promises them, "Open the doors or my wilderuckers will shred you."

The two adult wilderuckers race this way. The guards make up their minds in all of a moment, open the doors, and run. Ejjer marches in.

The inner keep is a lounge adorned with the finest materials and comforts. Ejjer finds Viceroy Rampapart meeting with the chair-lords over weapons and snake powder. There's a shrine— and a *tomb*. Ejjer is confused by it, but more so by the people— they all hold so still and are so shocked at seeing him that they don't even breathe when he takes a few steps forward for a closer look. The tomb is stone and carved with moments of battles Ward Harrol is known to have personally fought and won. A giant, stopped clock is embedded in one side, perhaps the only frozen clock in all of the continent. The king's clock. It is thick with crusty dust, and old. The name of the dead occupant is written in proud letters: Ward Harrol. Ejjer catches his breath and suddenly the viceroy and chair-lords snap out of their shock—they leap up as though caught in a crime. Ejjer has seen behind the curtain. "There is no king?"

Rampapart and the chair-lords look mortified. Ejjer laughs. "You're all carvers."

"Guards!" Rampapart screams, "GUARDS!"

Ejjer throws the baby wilderucker to Rampapart, who can't stop herself from instinctually catching it. The adult wilderuckers burst into the room. One bites Ejjer as the other chases Rampapart, who throws the baby monster. The chair-lords hurry for the doors—Ejjer leaps out and pulls them shut. He braces the doors and seals the chair-lords in. They scream inside as the wilderuckers howl and kill.

"Help me!" Ejjer hears Rampapart shout over and over. He hears a clattering, then a large explosion shakes the walls. He has no idea what could have caused that, what chemical plans were being experimented upon in that room and why, but the shouts persist and the wilderucker howls continue so much that he forgets all about the explosion.

Ejjer slides to the floor and looks at his bite wound. It's terrible. Infected already. He thinks about what's going on in that room, and how that violence is only happening because he tried to sever a family of beasts. Or is he not thinking about the wilderuckers, but rather Dancin and Rose? How love can cause such brutality is curious to him, and he wishes he had more time to ponder it. But he knows his wounds will overtake him too soon for that.

He leans back and smiles as the screams go on and on. He decides to bathe in a thought that pleases him, the thought that has driven all his dreams and fueled his tears. But he will have tears no more, because his destiny has come true, at last. He relishes getting to say it aloud, though no one is here to notice him. "I am a king. A *conquering* king. My sprawhammid is great. If only for a while." His conquered foes' screaming agony behind those doors is a symphony to him. He slips away, and in his final moments he realizes the truth, which I share with you now:

Ward Harrol died many years ago, but his inner circle kept him alive for their own reason: power.

In the public square, ashes dance in a faint breeze where the torture structure once stood, but is now an extinguished pyre. Countless bodies lie all over the place. In the shock of it all, Strelkie and Punimin have stopped fighting, traumatized by the sudden tragedy, and they dig through the debris and ashes together to help who they may.

Teacup helps rummage through the remains, and backs into a tiny boy flycub doing the same. He's got a tuft of hair on top of his head, the start of a mane that's still years away from coming in. He wears a broken collar, stamped with the name of his owner, a Strelkie collector of rare creatures, whose bottom half and top half have been separated by the explosion. Teacup licks his nose. He bites her ear. She swats his cheek. They suddenly run in circles around each other, then rub against each other. He tugs her tiny battle vest off and seems to laugh. She seems to scowl. A scrap of wood shifts under them and they slip—and they find Toir Pat, alive. They squawk and beat their wings and harness the attention from all around.

A Strelkie sneaks up on Teacup and her new rarest of friends, and tries to catch them, but they spring away together and fly into the air like mates. The boy knocks off Teacup's helmet midair, and they soar off into the sky and out of Strelkie city for good.

Toir Pat watches the two love cats escape as people tug him out of a heap of ruins and to his feet.

As for myself, I am the only rebel who survived Pistol Rose's sprawhammid. Everyone who knew of my betrayal died.

Toir Pat leads a group of Strelkie, and wary Punimin, to the king's temple, where they discover Ejjer's body. The doors are torn open. It's deathly quiet in that room.

I learned that day the viceroy and her governing chair-lords kept the chain of command limited to only themselves. They even made it illegal for anyone in the army to hold ruling power.

Toir Pat and his group look inside: the chair-lords have been ravaged dead. There was some kind of explosion in here, too, and burns on the walls that look tinged brown by snake powder. The wilderuckers were blown to pieces by whatever concoction the snake powder was being used to create. But there is no sign of Viceroy Rampapart—just her bloody bootprints leading away and outside.

So, without the leadership and without the judge, Pistol Rose's sprawhammid left me, the city's biggest defense lawyer, as the highest-ranking member of the law. And though the rebellion was outnumbered by loyal citizens, we had passionate people willing to join the invading Punimin and fight. And that's all that matters— one dog can herd a flock of sheep. Give me a thousand dogs, and I'll organize a country.

Toir Pat and his group are shocked by what they see in the room: Ward Harrol's tomb.

Convincing the Strelkie I should be their leader wasn't difficult at that point.

Toir Pat turns to the group. "Burn it."

As the king's temple burns, Toir Pat marches away with some Strelkie who follow as new loyalists.

An hour didn't pass before the shock of the explosion wore off, and the Punimin who managed to breach the city walls forgot about helping their fellow countrymen deal with the aftermath of the horrific explosion. They found themselves again at-throats with the Strelkie, again at war—but not all of the Strelkie. Not those who wished to set the city free. For the first time, those Strelkie stood side-by-side with Punimin.

Fighting breaks out all over the city, a civil war brawling in the streets with every manner of weapon, be them soldierly tools, or the trinkets and sales things people can get their hands on, or the broken glass of shop windows or stones pried loose from the alleyways, or the gears and limbs of unfortunate servant machines too near the action to avoid being plucked. And all of this frothy fighting is muddied and complicated by Punimin raging right and left and up and sideways, some of whom have worked in the city and know the roads, but many of whom have never been here before and have a difficult time thinking about fighting their Strelkie enemies while also taking in the distracting, splendid magnificence of the city all at once. The battle isn't citywide, but the places where it sloshes and slithers are like a toybox being shook until every person, item, fist and thing is rattled together in messy knots. Yet it is a glorious skirmish for the Punimin; not a wager of battle-skill discipline, for their plan after breaching the wall was never agreed upon, but for all of the Punimin it is a passionate release of riotous emotion and fumbling bursts of physical rage. For the breakaway Strelkie who join them and fight against their kingdom, it is a strangely welcome brotherhood where automatic friendships are bound in the thick of quick war. And for the Strelkie who stand against this revolution, be they soldiers or be they citizens, it is a frightening hellscape made of berserk madmen and violent women slashing through beautiful streets like glass shards on fabric—streets and shops and parks that mere moments ago represented the pinnacle of peaceful, controlled utopia. It's like a dam has burst and day suddenly has become a clock breaking and tearing itself apart with springs lurching wildly loose to shred whatever gets in the way, and gears spinning off and cutting fiercely as a brutal tantrum and a curse against its engineering. It is the release of an Age by a people starving for action to the point of desperate, near-thoughtless insanity.

Countless carvings will be made of the sloppy and true events of this day. Sculptings of fisticuffs will pile onto moments of heroic wrestlings and swordplay and gun bravery. Exaggerations will mount and outdo the next story on every history clock, and from here on, many Strelkie will take up the Punimin practice of calendaring the past with such whittling ways. But despite the glorious lenses through which many will look upon this day and add mirth to the menace, one truth will never be carved foul, never be bullied into brighter light than it is, or rendered with an embarrassed hand to a false improvement—the rebellion flag with a scrap of The Bride's wedding dress will be remembered upon every clock history exactly as it is seen today, for to the hearts and eyes and memories of those who hate it, it is seared into their lives and impossible to misremember; for the people who follow it and welcome it and need it, it is already perfect.

They called it the "Two Hour War." It took much longer to quell the Punimin invaders, but two hours is where most of the remembered fighting took place, and the Strelkie who resisted the turning tide would continue to fight hard to belittle its length. For the Punimin, that shortness would become exaggerated the other way, with some calling it the "Two Minute War," to boast about how quickly the Strelkie kingdom fell to them—though it didn't exactly fall. That day, in those hours, it was simply wounded, though wounded by poison that would not leave.

Knowing which Strelkie wanted a rebellion, and which wanted the old ways to return, was impossible to sort. Fear and doubt and dread filled the veins of every Strelkie. No one could safely tell friend or foe simply by looking at them. No Strelkie could trust another, and certainly none could trust the Punimin workers on whom they so vitally depended. The "unity" Ward Harrol's chair-lords had hammered so hard into place via edicts and bedrooms and hierarchies and threats was wholly destroyed in those two hours by the people themselves, and everyone knew it. When the battle finally ended and the streets grew quiet, everyone knew.

Angry Strelkie watch Toir Pat walk by in the aftermath of the battle, through the shattered streetways and up-piling bodies of the dead. Toir Pat, their unelected leader, their controversial new king.

I called for all crimes of the day to be forgiven, and I reversed the law imposing the Strelkie soldiers to live among the Punimin; their place was to be in the city. Many Strelkie hated me for that. Many Strelkie wanted to punish Punimin for the crimes of Pistol Rose and her attack on Strelkie society. And they always would. Unofficial wars began across the country in scattered battles and chaotic skirmishes, largely without battleplans. Our forts suffered heavy losses, and many Punimin villages burned. Both sides claimed "sprawhammid" as their own rallying cry. Eventually these hostilities died down as people turned their attention to their own lives, rather than the life the state would dictate, and though there ran a wild ubiquity of differences among the mouthy elites, and canyons of disagreement between everyone else, getting along fell in vogue and become the way. Perhaps this happened because of how I ruled? Perhaps despite of it. I used the word "sprawhammid" too, but to mean "the personal quest for meaning," and I carved the word into every new law I made and every old law I outlawed. Some people despised that, but as ruler of the continent I felt I had the right to fix the meaning of the word in place, and since I had more than a little to do with the brief Punimin invasion that was fueled by the word, I felt some ownership over its future.

To some, that invasion, that betrayal of country, is what made me such a prized, strong and brilliant unifying leader—in that revolution brings many together, especially when that many aim to seize power for themselves and those who agree with them. I was beloved because I represented the will of the people. To others, to those many who lost and who wished for the old ways of Strelkie dominance and Punimin oppression, or as they would call it, "a peaceful and natural balance," that so obviously worked for them, I was a treasonous, foolishly stupid, swine-minded cud unworthy of my ruling station entirely, and a weak, scandal-clad scoundrel who didn't one bit represent the will of the people and who damaged our country beyond repair.

In other words, I was a typical king.

And I would be carving to say I didn't enjoy it. I now regret the enjoying, because I think it's what made me so typical. A fair king would have found a way to help all the people, not just the ones who managed to rise up and place him in power through threats and blood. Under my reign, Strelkie society actually expanded to the rest of the continent—there had always been forts and soldiers spread about the coasts, but before the revolution the Punimin wood dunes and ranges and peninsulas existed with few bothers from Strelkiedom—I saw to it to brush the people of both sides together, in an effort to erase sides. I kept the birthing hospitals on the Line, but outlawed examiners so no one would be assigned to Punimin or Strelkie. This of course led to mothers deciding for themselves, and Strelkie began to beget only Strelkie, and Punimin only Punimin. This did not help erase the "sides;" it only furthered their divide. A fair king might have found a better way. A fair king might have built more cities, or torn down the walls of the one we had. A fair king would have known what to do. But, regardless of the history read or the life witnessed, no one can honestly say we've ever had a fair king in all of the known Ages. Some kings have at least been better than chair-lord counsels on one side, and mobs on the other, and the clock carvings I've seen generally put me in that camp, much to the pride of my friends. When all is said and done, the opinions of friends are all one seems to have left to count on outside of one's own *conscience. And kinging is a killer of conscience, so I am most glad for my friends.*

Now in a humble church set in a sunny wilderness, Toir Pat sits in a chair before an altar. He has become old. He says, "I did try to heal, not just the wounds I opened but the ones that predated me. And the war that was borne of that controversial day was blessedly short, but my reign was not enough god for some, and too much king for others. Politics. I made some lasting changes to King's Law, and today the Strelkie and Punimin live, not with a strong peace, but with a strong understanding. I can live with that, but I can't live as an indulgent old king. So, after a time I resigned, and left the city, and joined you fine Punimin here in the deep forest—where for some reason you make me officiate these things."

This is a wedding for a fresh-faced young couple and their Punimin guests. Pleasant flowerful decorations are everywhere. Toir Pat stands. "That's the story of *Pistol Rose and the Wedding That Sparked a War.* She and Clock Dancin, and their brave families, are why you are able to be married today, in the freeness of sunlight." He hands the young groom a pistol, and the bride a clock. He proudly wraps up his duty: "You have gathered with me to hear the story of Pistol Rose ... and the trouble she made. The war that sprung from her wedding was among the greatest sprawhammids in known history. It ended the Fifth Age and began the Sixth. For better or for worse. Now, you have come for the story, and the story having been told, it becomes yours to continue. May your troubles be worth it and more. This is my last wedding before I retire. So, with the power vested in me ..."

The groom clips the pistol onto the bride. Toir Pat continues, "By the one true God ..."

The bride clips the clock onto the groom.

"I now pronounce you wed," Toir Pat says with a nearly blushing smile. The bride and groom kiss. The guests happily rave and applaud. Toir Pat has to shout over them, "May their hearts live forever and be storied!"

All respond, "Storied forever!"

Toir Pat starts to leave, an old man in a hurry for other business—but the bride catches him. "Toir Pat? We have to know."

The groom insists. "You couldn't have been the only survivor. The explosion was dreadful, but if you escaped it, why couldn't the Pistols and the Clocks?"

Toir Pat razzes him. "Are you calling me a liar?"

The groom shakes his head. "There are many Pistol Rose stories—"

Toir Pat chuckles. "And snake powder came from Viceroy Rampapart. And the continents drifted together. And the Dead Assassins can't be killed. And I'm seven feet tall. Legends invented by carvers."

The bride whispers, "But the secret to good carving is telling the truth. We understand the families would have had to go into hiding, to Afar. I heard that you became dear friends with the Pistols and Clocks and took secret holidays as king to visit them there many times—"

Toir Pat politely takes her by the hands. "Afar? Me? Dear, this was all a long time ago, a great many years, and no one has ever found the Jungle Country. There's nowhere in the world to hide like that. Afar doesn't exist. Those who try to cross the Beast Sea and live, return wailing of boar krakens—and worse. Pistol Rose and Clock Dancin are gone."

The groom's face falls. "So, they didn't make it?"

Toir Pat puts his hands on their shoulders. "But you will. That's the story now."

They smile softly. He puts his hands on their cheeks. "That's the story." Their smiles brighten as they put their thoughts on their own road and adventures ahead.

Music and a party break out. The bride and groom dance their first dance, and their new life begins. Toir Pat watches with satisfied eyes, shakes some guests' hands, and quietly slips away as the celebration turns boisterous and rowdy, as all Punimin parties seem to do.

The Blood Sea is warm today. The water is black-red, and violent with waves as ever. I row a small boat away from a five-sailed Kraken Hunter's ship in the distance. They always let me journey with them, because I've never told them my real name. They think I am merely a retired scribe in search of God, in search of love, in search of meaning greater than myself. Just like them. They call this searching "sprawhammid," and I like the uncomplicated peace with which they say it. It doesn't mean to them what it came to mean in my younger years. Had they known I am Toir Pat, they never once would have brought me to this jungle island—they help protect it from those who would bring fame, and infamy, and carvings of any kind. They would've handed me over to the Pirate Sisters.

Children play on the beach, watched by their parents. They hurry to help me climb ashore with strong arms and compliments. I've brought two large bouquets of flowers. By the treeline are two graves. I lay the flowers there, for my friends. Were we friends? I feel like we were after my having told this story for so many years. And these are the exact words I've been saying for ages, letter for letter, as I see it. It lives before my eyes with every blink and with every fall to my bed pillow. I see it again in my mind as I chat with some natives who have agreed to let me stay in their Jungle Country, Afar. I see every detail of my tale, even the lie.

But the truth about this story ...

Forgive me for a moment while I kiss the two headstones. This is where Clock Wyatt and Pistol Jennifer are laid to rest. I look up the shore. Two grandparents sit watching the water from a straw bench. They wave at me. I wave back with a smile. I know them.

Where was I? Ah, the truth, the truth about Pistol Rose and Clock Dancin, who died that day, a lifetime ago at the executioner's platform, is ...

I'm caught off guard by Clock Zoe and her husband. How grown she's gotten since my first visit to this place. And here is Pistol Beau with a family of his own, populated by wonderful natives from this land. Those two watching grandparents rise from their seat, hold hands, and walk to me.

Now the truth about Rose and Dancin, as I was saying, and for the first time I share, is this:

Yes. They made it. They found their true sprawhammid in this place of peace.

The grandparents hug me. My friends. Time has taken them, Rose and Dancin, on a journey as storied as mine; we have much to share—the tales of the final years of my kingship for me, and for them, the grim and daring and heroic tales and travels of the family they made, some adventures of which I partially know already, some of which I fear to learn because of the frightful rumors I've heard.

The year is now 54 of the Sixth Age, setting me at 104—a number old enough that I feel no shame for finally settling my journeys at last, and carving them with ink and paper. But, given the medicines reserved for kings and their company, of which as a matter of law I partook, my age is still young enough that I have time to live somewhat more, and somewhat well, here with my friends. At last, we are together for all of our days to come.

May we find sprawhammid as Rose and Dancin. May we feel our tales as alive, and now. Never as history, never fading, and always as one with us. May our hearts live forever and be storied.

Storied forever.

The Anthem of Ash & Pistols continues with Book II:

Pistol Tiffin and the Prophecy Killer

michaelryanhahn.com

Made in the USA
Columbia, SC
02 September 2023

22347901R00115